'Robbed of Sleep'

Stories to Stay Up For, Volume 1

Edited by Troy Blackford

Table of Contents

Introduction

You know what this is, don't you? It's an idea sandwich. It's a strange lexical capsule which will not just transport but veritably *fling* you from wherever you are to places you never could be, and to more than a few where you never, ever want to go. It's a meeting of the minds — not just minds of the ragtag assortment of authors gathered here, but of all of their minds with yours.

It won't be easy. This book will challenge your imagination, strain your sense of refinement, stretch the boundaries of your disbelief, and possibly infuriate you with its unwillingness to bend to the rules. But one thing it won't do, dear reader, is bore you. Whether you come along with these authors on a hunt for a mystic dryad, a trip to a deadly circus, a tropical getaway — in the sense of desperate escape, not a relaxing cruise — or on a one-way bus ride to Other Land, a ride with a noisome girlfriend, or even just a plain old descent into madness, you will most certainly be leaving the trappings of ordinary life behind.

Even if just for a moment.

And isn't momentary escape the *point* of short stories? Not escape as in 'escape from life,' but the kind of escape a rocket makes when it leaves the boundaries of earth behind and heads into orbit. We're not here to help you escape from the problems of your life, we're here to help you escape *into* something that lies *beyond* your life, even if it's just for a fleeting instant. And if you forget your bills and your chores and all that rot while you're out there, that's fine with us.

We sure weren't thinking about *our* chores while we wrote these. It was a pretty good feeling. We'd love to spread it around. So hop on board!

Be prepared to be stretched past the breaking point of credulity; bruised with raw weird; rammed full of painful possibilities—and most of all, get ready to be *Robbed of Sleep*, because, ladies and gentleman, boys and girls, these really are *Stories to Stay Up For*.

-Troy Blackford
Your Humble Editor and Lowly Contributor
June 2014, While the Stars Do Shine

'PVC Ceremony'

by Val Tenterhosen

I hate when people try digging outside your house without asking you for permission. The same thing happened to me, like, virtually every single time I tried to have dirt outside my house. I don't know what the people wanted with it. They said they had buried pipes out there, but I would have appreciated some kind of heads up about that.

I didn't know I was buying a house with a bunch of pipes stuck down in the yard. But that's the way things are these days. It's a collection of pigs and all you can do is keep pouring and pouring and hoping some light comes out in the end. It never does, but you can keep hoping and so that's what I do. So when they look through my pipes, I get real nervous.

I get real nervous so I start doing my thing and then before you know it I have to bury even *more* of them between the pipes and the whole cycle starts up again. It's a real wreck.

So yeah: whenever they get sniffing around my pipes, I get plenty nervous. You would too. Come to think of it, so would they.

Oh well. That's just the way the world is these days. You get used to it.

That's just how it works.

'The Other Land Express'

by Todd Keisling

The jostling Greyhound roused Gregory Simmons from a doze. He shifted in his seat, realizing that his music had stopped, and when he checked his iPod he discovered the battery was dead.

Figures, he thought. He'd left his charger back at his old man's place. The AC adapter was still plugged into the wall socket next to his bed, one of the few belongings he'd left behind in haste, and he didn't have enough cash left to buy a new one.

So much for that. He coiled his ear buds, stuffed the iPod into his backpack, and leaned his head against the window, watching as the world rolled past in a darkened blur. Miles away, lightning arced across a cloudbank, turning the hills into silhouettes, and his thoughts into fears.

What if his old man came after him? Unlikely, but plausible. Then again, Gregory doubted his old man had even noticed he was gone. These days, the only time Eddie Simmons paid him any attention was when he wanted a beer or when he wanted to beat on his son.

Light from a passing car filled the cabin, and for an instant Gregory saw his reflection in the glass. The bruises were still fresh, but the swelling had gone down. That was good. People wouldn't be so keen to notice or stare. The last thing he needed was for some Good Samaritan to ask if he's okay, why he's traveling, where his parents are, and so on.

In Gregory's rush to escape from his father's apartment, he'd not given much thought to a cover story should a stranger inquire about his travels. "Traveling to visit my mom" seemed too cliché; "Traveling to my mom's funeral" was far more accurate, even if it was just a few years too late. Both stories made his heart hurt for the same reason.

No one bothered to ask, though. It was a fact which might have irritated him under different circumstances, but today he was grateful for the anonymity. Today he was a seventeen-year-old nobody, just another kid with fresh bruises on the run from the bad cards life had dealt him. A couple hundred miles back, his father was probably arriving home with a fresh buzz from the pub, the old bastard's knuckles still raw, ignorant of Gregory's absence or the money missing from beneath his mattress.

His father's drunken slurs echoed in his head: *Should'a kicked yer ass out years ago, ya worthlesh punk. Yer a parasite, thash what you are. A worthless faggot parasite.*

The old man's words always did more harm than his fists, but years of suffering through both had tempered Gregory's wits, and he wouldn't let himself be frightened into returning home. Eddie Simmons crossed a line this time, and Gregory had had enough.

A bolt of lightning lit up the night, fracturing the skyline into a thousand jagged pieces. Gregory's bruised reflection stared back from the window, and he was about to turn away when something else caught his eye: the reflection of a man sitting in the seat across the aisle. He was staring at Gregory.

Or *was* he? Gregory couldn't tell, and the lightning had ceased by the time he looked over his shoulder. There was only a bus filled with shadows, its occupants marked as silhouettes against the glare of headlights from passing cars. The man across the aisle turned his head slightly and offered a short nod.

Gregory returned the nod instinctively, more as a reaction than out of good manners, and turned back toward the window. Heat flooded Gregory's cheeks, and he tried holding his breath to slow his thudding heart. What if the stranger knew he was a runaway? What if Gregory had given something away in his appearance or maybe even through his mannerisms?

Stop it, he told himself. *The guy's just being nice. You're the one who turned around and stared, remember?*

He glanced back across the aisle. The stranger had turned away, staring out the window at the passing storm. Gregory leaned his head against the window and closed his eyes. *Just my imagination. The real monster's a few hundred miles back. Keep it cool until the next stop. Call Tommy when you get there. He'll be worried. Just don't draw attention to yourself.*

The thought of his boyfriend — Was he a boyfriend? Could he call Tommy that now? — set his heart at ease, but the lingering fear that this stranger somehow knew what he was doing kept Gregory awake for the next fifty miles.

* * *

The phone rang three times before a voice said, "Hello?"

"Hey Tommy, it's me."

"Greg? Are you okay?"

The surprise in Tommy Keegan's voice made him smile. "Yeah. A little bruised, but the old man's done worse. I missed you."

His cheeks flushed. Speaking those words aloud filled him with a giddiness he'd not felt since he was a child, and the smile on his face felt so alien he didn't recognize the sensation at first. His stomach tumbled and rolled, held adrift by the butterflies inside, finally free of the stone he'd carried. He *missed* him.

Gregory was so caught up in his elation that he didn't notice the long pause on the other end of the line.

"Tommy? You still there?"

"Yeah, Greg. I'm here. Listen, I'm not supposed to talk to you anymore. My mom . . . well, your dad called my mom after, you know. She knows all about us. About what we were doing."

That familiar heat clung to Gregory's cheeks, but for different reasons. No matter how far he ran, he couldn't escape his father's shadow.

"You don't . . . regret what we did, do you?"

"No. Yes. I don't know, Greg. I'm just confused, y'know? I mean, I don't even know you, and you're on the other side of the country. It was fun chatting with you online, but now things are so serious, y'know? I think I just need some time to get my head straight."

Gregory didn't know how to respond. The elation he'd felt only moments before had completely drained from him, and the butterflies in his gut had all but flown away. He felt as though he'd taken one of his dad's sucker punches, his lungs deflated, his head lost in a daze. The bruise on his cheek throbbed. He squeezed the payphone against his ear and leaned against the wall.

"You don't mean that, Tommy."

8

"I think I do, Greg. We're just names in a chat room, man. It's not like we'll ever meet face to face. We just met the wrong people, is all."

He squeezed the receiver until his knuckles popped. *The wrong people*. Those were his father's words. A voice boomed overhead from a loudspeaker, announcing the next bus was boarding. Gregory ignored the call; it wasn't his bus.

"What was that? Greg, where are you?"

Gregory clenched his teeth as his vision went cloudy with tears. "It doesn't matter. I'm sorry I bothered you, Tommy. I'm sorry—"

—*I ever met you*, but he didn't say it. The words hung there on his tongue, weighted down by the pointless anger of heartbreak. He closed his eyes, trying to hold back the flood building up behind them. His face burned.

"Don't be like this," Tommy said, but Gregory was already hanging up the phone. Just before he set the receiver back in its cradle, he thought he heard Tommy say they could still be friends. That was a lie, though, just like everything else had been.

Gregory slung his backpack over his shoulder, wiped his eyes, and found a quiet corner at the far end of the terminal. He sat down, drew his knees to his chest, and allowed the levy to break behind his eyes. The flood waters rose. He hoped he would drown in them.

* * *

Tommy had only ever asked once about Gregory's family. After a few months of chatting online, they'd swapped phone numbers so they'd have a voice to match their text. Gregory's father was still working third shift, so he had free reign of the phone in the late hours—which was great, because Tommy lived on the west coast where everything was three hours behind. Gregory missed those early days. He slept better.

"There's not much to say. My mom died of cancer a few years ago. And my dad . . ."

As far as Gregory was concerned, his real father had died in an accident after he was born. That's what he told himself to deal with the monster wearing his father's face. When he was younger he made up stories about how his real father died while committing a heroic act, like saving a group of children from a burning orphanage. Sometimes he told people his real father died in a car accident. And sometimes, when he was feeling particularly cynical, he told people the truth: the man he lived with really was his father. Sometimes, when the old bastard had had enough to drink, Eddie Simmons beat on his son to make himself feel better.

That first night they spoke, Gregory chose to be honest with his friend.

"Your old man sounds like a real asshole."

"He is," Gregory said. "One day I'm going to pack up and leave."

"You could always come out here," Tommy said. "We've got a spare bedroom. It would be nice to meet you face to face."

Gregory smiled. "I'd like that."

After a long pause, Tommy let out an exasperated sigh. "I think I would, too."

Their calls were infrequent at first, only once or twice a week, but as their relationship grew, so did their desire to speak to one another. Tommy asked his mom for a webcam for his birthday, and Gregory managed to scrape together enough spare cash to buy a cheap camera for himself. The resolution was shitty, but he could finally see Tommy's face, and that gave him something to look forward to every day.

Looking back, Gregory knew that was the beginning of something he wished he'd never started. The low ache in his cheek—and the pain he felt in his heart whenever he thought of Tommy—simply wasn't worth it. Now he was stranded in a bus terminal hundreds of miles from home, caught between two dead ends.

* * *

"You okay, son?"

Gregory opened his eyes, squinting at the dark figure standing over him. He squeezed the strap of his backpack to make sure it was still there.

"Dangerous, you know." The stranger stepped back and offered his hand. "Sleeping in the terminal, I mean. All manner of folk come through here at all hours. Lost and found, they all come through here."

He eyed the stranger's gesture with caution. After a moment his vision cleared, and Gregory saw the man's odd face with harsh clarity. The stranger wore a dusty old suit with fraying seams. He was older, with shiny salt and pepper hair slicked back and tucked behind his ears. The skin of his face was leathery, stretched tight over bone, and his eyes were like two gray pearls submerged in darkened sands.

"I'm fine," Gregory said, licking his lips. His gaze fell upon a pair of soda machines on the other side of the terminal. How much money did he have left? He couldn't remember.

The stranger twiddled his fingers in the air. "I won't bite. Just want to help."

Gregory hesitated a moment longer before taking the man's hand. The stranger helped him to his feet. "Thanks," he said, looping his arm through the backpack's strap. He checked his iPod for the time, but remembered the battery was dead. He looked at the strange man with the sunken eyes. "Do you have the time?"

The stranger pulled back his sleeve and checked his watch. "Quarter past two. You were asleep for an hour."

Gregory nodded, took two steps, and stopped. He turned and looked back at the man with the leathery face.

"What did you say?"

"You were asleep for an hour. I was watching from over there." He pointed to a bench fifteen feet away. "Here's some advice if you're going to run: You can't be invisible to everyone all the time. Someone's always watching." The stranger held out his hand. "Name's John."

Gregory gaped in stunned silence. His first impulse was to tell this man with the weird face to piss off, but there was distinct calm in John's voice that disarmed Gregory's mental alarms. John didn't mean him any harm; if he did, he would've already made his move while Gregory slept. That thought gave Gregory some comfort.

He reached out and shook John's hand. "I'm Greg."

"Greg, it's a pleasure to meet you. Always nice to meet another wayward soul at a bus terminal. By the look of you, I'd say your reasons for running are about as good as they get."

The flush of Gregory's cheeks prompted his bruise to throb, and he put his hand to his face instinctively. "Yeah," he said. "Nice to meet you, too."

John nodded. "I'm sorry, son. I don't mean to offend, but that is quite a shiner you've got."

Gregory blushed. "It's . . . it's a long story."

"Hey, I understand. Listen, we have a rule where I come from: always look forward. Never mind what happened. It's in the past so let it stay there, you know?" John pulled back his sleeve and took a look at his watch. His knuckles were badly wrinkled, almost as if he'd suffered severe burns in the past. "I've got about an hour to kill before my ride shows up. What do you say I buy you a snack?"

Gregory reached into his pocket and frowned at the loose collection of nickels and dimes. Sixty cents in total. He met John's gaze and nodded. "All right," he said. "You're on, mister."

"Wonderful," John said, his leathery face wrinkling at his cheeks.

Gregory followed his newfound friend across the lonely terminal, picked out something from the vending machine, and sat down on a nearby bench. He opened his pack of crackers and took a bite. John watched with unblinking curiosity. The way the stranger stared with those sunken eyes unnerved him, and he had a sudden flash of recognition: the man on the bus.

Gregory swallowed too fast, wincing as the bits of cracker

scratched the back of his throat. He coughed, spraying crumbs across the floor. John chuckled.

"Not all at once, son."

"Sorry," Gregory rasped. He cleared his throat. "Where did you say you were headed again?"

John smiled. "I didn't."

"Oh."

"Is there something you want to ask me?"

Gregory took another bite of cracker, but not because he was hungry. No, the feeling of hunger had passed moments before, displaced by a leaden weight in his gut. Heat clung to his cheeks now, threatening to suffocate him as he struggled to find the right words. *Be cool*, a voice spoke in his mind. *Just be cool.*

There *was* something he wanted to ask this strange man, and the words were right there, ready to be given voice, but he was so afraid. He felt like he was in the presence of his father, too afraid to speak, too afraid to *move*.

John put his hand on Gregory's shoulder. "I won't bite, Greg."

Gregory chewed the cracker and swallowed. He took a breath. "Are you the man who was staring at me on the bus?"

"Of course I am."

John spoke so matter-of-factly, so disarmingly that Gregory almost accepted the statement without question—but the look in the stranger's eye was too gleeful and eager to set his mind at ease. A chill crawled down the back of Gregory's neck.

"You—you were watching me?"

"I was."

"So you followed me?"

"Only as far back as the last stop. You caught my eye immediately. I know a runner when I see one, son. Old John Doe used to be one himself."

Gregory blinked. "John Doe? Seriously?"

"Yes, sir." He rose to his feet and offered Gregory a short bow. "A genuine Nobody, at your service."

Gregory squeezed the strap of his backpack. All of his belongings were in the pack, and if he needed to run—and he might—he didn't want to leave them all behind. Not that keeping the backpack would do him much good; aside from his ID, all he had was a change of clothes, an empty wallet, and a dead iPod.

"Relax," John Doe said, recognizing the boy's apprehension. "I'm not going to hurt you."

"Isn't that what you *would* say if you were going to hurt me?"

"Touché." John returned to his seat, leaving a wide space between them. Gregory gripped the backpack, ready to run at the first sign of trouble. "Despite what you may think of me, I have helped thousands of others suffering from the same plight as you."

Gregory scoffed. "Same plight? Mister, you don't even know me."

"This is true," John Doe said. He reached up and scratched

at his face. The flesh around his eye sagged from the pressure, and made a strange squelching sound which twisted Gregory's stomach into knots. "But what I do know is enough. I know your name is Gregory Simmons. I know that you're on the run from your father because he beats you on a daily basis, and last night he went a little too far because he caught you masturbating to your boyfriend over the internet." John Doe smiled, revealing yellowed teeth and spotted gums. "Would you say that's enough? Or should I go on?"

An icy serpent coiled around his insides, squeezing the last breath of air from Gregory's lungs. He exhaled in a low, raspy heave as the cloud of heat returned to his face. He suddenly felt like a small child lost in the wilderness, yearning for the comfort of his home no matter how broken it was. And yet here he was, hundreds of miles from his comfort zone, facing the real world head on for the first time — and feeling helplessly terrified.

Gregory stared into John Doe's sunken eyes. "Who are you?" He swallowed back the ball of cotton in his throat. "*What* are you?"

"I told you, Greg. I'm a genuine Nobody. I help all the other Nobodies get from here to there, and sometimes I find Nobodies who don't realize they're Nobodies. Sometimes I find people who want to *become* Nobodies just like the rest of us."

"I don't understand," Gregory said. He shook his head. "What do you mean you're nobody?"

"Ask yourself something, son. Where are you going to go after tonight? Back to your father's home? Or to your boyfriend's house? Neither one of them want you. All you have is a pocket full of loose change and a bus ticket to the west coast."

He turned away. "How do you know that? This doesn't make any sense, you fucking weirdo."

"I know because it's my business to know. Because it's my part to play. I help others disappear, and sometimes that means finding those who don't realize they want to. People like you, I can almost smell your desperation. It's like overripe fruit, just a bit too sweet and slightly off. No one wants you the way you are. So I'll ask you again, son: where are you going to go?"

He dropped his smile and stared. Gregory looked down at his backpack, running his fingers across the fabric of the strap while a number of sarcastic replies ran through his mind. What could he say? He hadn't considered Tommy backtracking on everything, and he'd not yet given himself time to grieve over that particular loss. Going back home wasn't an option now, especially since he'd stolen his old man's rainy day savings to buy a one-way bus ticket to the west coast. He could already hear Eddie Simmons screaming

(*worthless*

faggot

parasite)

loud enough to shake the heavens. Like it or not, he was on his own now, and this strange man with the squelching face had a point: no one wanted him. He wished his mom was still alive. She might've been upset over what he'd been doing with Tommy, but she wouldn't have hit him. She would've made an effort to understand.

But that didn't matter now because she'd been dead for years. Now he was alone, and no one wanted him. No one except Mr. Doe.

John checked his watch. "In about five minutes, a bus full of other Nobodies is going to pull up to the station and I'm going to climb aboard. If you come with me, no one's going to ask for your ticket. You'll be welcomed. If you join me, Greg, I can make you two promises." He climbed to his feet and held out a wrinkled, leathery hand. "The first is that you can be whomever you want to be, and no one will judge you for what you choose."

Gregory wiped tears from his eyes and looked up at John Doe. "And the second?"

"The second is that everything you are now will never be again. Gregory Simmons will cease to exist. Who you become afterward is up to you, but you can never be you again."

He took John Doe's hand and rose to his feet. "You mean I'll have a new identity? New ID, name, address?"

John Doe smiled, and his lips clicked when they slid across his teeth. "Something like that."

* * *

The bus arrived on time, just as John Doe said it would, and a voice filled the terminal from a series of loudspeakers announcing its departure time. They had ten minutes to board. Gregory stood with his companion on the sidewalk, shivering in the breeze. The storm had let up over an hour ago but the damp air carried a chill that nipped at his ears.

John Doe took a breath. "Last chance to change your mind, son. Once you board the Other Land Express, you can't go back. Everything changes from here on out."

"You were right," Gregory said. He clenched his jaws to

keep his teeth from chattering. "When you said no one wants me the way I am. I don't know how you knew, but you were right. There's nothing waiting for me now."

"Have you thought about where you'll go?"

He hadn't, but the answer came easily enough. "I'd still like to visit the west coast. See the ocean. You know, where it's warm."

"West coast it is, then." John Doe held up his hand and the bus door folded open. He stepped across the sidewalk and stuck his head inside. "Just two tonight, Joe." He turned back and motioned to Gregory. "Right this way, Mr. Simmons."

Gregory slipped his arms through the straps of his backpack and frowned. "Don't call me that," he said. "That's my father's name."

John Doe nodded. "My apologies, Greg. After tonight, you won't have to worry about that anymore."

A series of overhead dome lights stretched to the back of the bus, illuminating rows of smiling faces. Men and women of varying ages filled the cabin, and despite the poor lighting, Gregory saw their eyes were sunken into their skulls just like his strange host. He followed John Doe down the aisle toward the back of bus, and as he moved, several of the other Nobodies turned to watch. They whispered among themselves, nodding in acceptance if he caught their gaze, with their thin lips peeled back to reveal rows upon rows of yellowed, brittle teeth.

After he found a seat near the back, Gregory realized his heart was racing, and he wasn't sure if it was from fear or excitement. He thought about what he would tell Tommy, but his heart sank when he remembered how their last conversation had gone. And what was it that John Doe had said? He wouldn't be himself after this?

Not that he'd want to pay Tommy a visit anyway. Even though Gregory's heart ached, somewhere deep down he knew Tommy lacked conviction. Gregory wasn't ashamed of what he'd done. It felt good and right, and he'd do it again if given the chance. He wished his old man was there so he could say it to his face.

But all that will be behind me, he thought. *It's time to look forward.*

John Doe took a seat across the aisle. He raised his hand again, and the bus shuddered into gear. The driver, Joe, came over the loudspeaker. "Good evening, fellow Nobodies. We've got some miles to go before our next stop, but before we make our way through the Other Lands, please put your hands together for our newcomer, Greg. He's the latest to join our tribe!"

Gregory looked at John and mouthed, *Tribe?*

John winked and joined in the applause. "Welcome, Gregory!"

A pair of older men turned in their seats and congratulated him. "We've been Nobodies for more than a decade," they said. "We joined together, and we make the exchange every few years. It's great to shed the skin. You'll love it!"

Gregory offered a polite smile, unsure of what to say. Joe's voice boomed from the speaker above: "Now you all know the rules: no shedding until we've crossed the boundary lines. We've got a long stretch through the Other Lands tonight, so that means you've got more time to make your exchange. Until then, find someone you like, someone who's your type, and get to know them. And remember, people: John Doe gets dibs on the newcomer."

He turned to John Doe once more, but his strange friend was conversing with a pair of young women in front of him. Gregory sank back into his seat and watched with mounting trepidation as the bus terminal grew smaller in the distance. Soon the bus was back on the highway, headed west toward America's enigmatic Other Lands.

* * *

They were on the road for an hour before John called out to him. Gregory lifted his head from the window pane and looked across the aisle at Mr. Doe's silhouette.

"We're almost there," John said. He shuffled across the aisle and sat next to Gregory. "Before we get there, I need to explain something."

Gregory sat up in his seat and rubbed his eyes. He'd almost dozed off, lulled to slumber by the rock and hum of the Greyhound. "What is it?"

John Doe leaned forward and rubbed his hands absently, his head bowed as if in prayer. "The Other Lands are a special place. Things are different there."

"Different how?"

"Different… in a lot of ways. You'll see it. More importantly, you'll feel it. It's like being drunk. Your senses are numbed. This place is where you'll become someone else."

Gregory leaned over and whispered into John's ear, "Are

you going to tell me what the hell is going on? Whatever it was that Joe was talking about back at the station?"

"I'm getting to that," John said. "But I think it may be best to show you. Do you feel that?"

He wasn't sure what John was talking about at first, but the sensation that came over him a moment later told him all he needed to know. He lost the feeling in his lips and tongue, followed by the tips of his nose and ear lobes. His fingertips tingled, and his toes were tickled with dozens of phantom pinpricks. Gregory blinked lazily, marveling at the strange, purple glow spreading across the sky.

Outside, the highway melted into an alien landscape pockmarked with gray craters and dotted with maroon vegetation. Trees curved from the earth like tentacles, their branches writhing with wildlife too small to be seen, but somehow Gregory could sense them, could almost see the vibration of their tiny wings beating the air. He remembered something Tommy had said about experiencing acid for the first time, and he wondered if John Doe had drugged him somehow.

"Is this—"

"It's real," John said. His lips peeled back into another toothy grin. "This is where the Nobodies of the world come to commune, Greg. Out here, we get to frolic backstage while the world carries on with its self-importance and loathing. Out here in the Other Lands, we're free to be ourselves."

The bus slowed to a stop in the middle of the gray desert. As if on cue, the passengers erupted into cries of jubilation. The two men in front embraced, while the women across the aisle kissed. Gregory looked marveled at the landscape, wondering how such a place could ever exist, and he was so caught up in the sensations in his body that he didn't notice the articles of clothing flying through the air.

John Doe rose from his seat and raised his hand to calm everyone.

"Friends and fellow Nobodies, tonight we inaugurate a new face into our tribe. He's a little nervous, but I think that once we strip off our earthly burdens, he'll feel right at home. After all, we're all the same beneath the flesh!"

What happened next left Gregory's mind reeling, and for the first few terrifying moments he questioned what he was seeing. The other passengers climbed out of their seats and stripped out of the remains of their clothing. Their naked silhouettes were cast in the dim, purple glow of the world beyond, and when the dome lights came on, Gregory saw that John Doe had joined them.

"Let me show you," John said. "Let me show you how to shed the old you."

So he did, and Gregory did everything he could not to scream.

John reached up, found a seam behind his ear, and peeled back the mask of his face, revealing the sinuous meat and muscle beneath. He lifted underneath his chin and yanked, stripping the flap of his face from his skull with a single motion. The sound that met Gregory's ears reminded him of Velcro, and the gaping stare of John Doe's skinless face made his stomach crawl into itself.

He watched in sickening horror as John Doe peeled back every bit of himself like a piece of fruit, moving on to his arms and hands, then on to his chest, gut, and groin. Every fold of skin peeled away with that same scratchy, squelching Velcro sound, and now Gregory understood the odd noise he'd heard back at the bus station.

He looked away from the stranger and recoiled in disgust as he witnessed others doing the same. The men in the next row helped each other peel away their flesh, one working his hands under the wrinkles and folds of the other, inching the skin away from the meat underneath like stripping back a sticker from plastic. The women across the aisle were already exposed. They ran their hands across their sinuous folds, exploring their anatomy, and Gregory realized with sickening horror that he couldn't tell if they were smiling anymore because their lips were gone.

"This is what it is to shed your skin," John said, offering his hand. "We come here to the Other Lands to strip away our burdens and trade faces. Here, we are free to be whomever we wish. Tonight, you will become me, Gregory. And I will become you. Forever one with the Nobody Tribe."

Gregory's mind buzzed. Was this what he wanted? Was this the price had to pay to become someone else?

John Doe slicked his leathery tongue across the top of his brittle teeth. "Remember what I told you, Greg. It's too late to go back, but I promise you'll thank me when it's over. I keep my promises."

Gregory reached out and took John Doe's hand for the last time. "Will I remember anything? Will it hurt?"

"You'll remember everything." John squeezed Gregory's hand. "And yes, my friend, it will hurt. The pain will be transcendent, the most glorious thing you have ever felt in your life."

John Doe's fingers sank into the boy's flesh, and Gregory knew his friend wasn't lying.

* * *

One day later, a man no one had ever seen before stepped off an unmarked Greyhound bus in Long Beach. He wore a dusty black suit that was nearly a size too big, and his youthful eyes betrayed the mess of salt and pepper hair sitting atop his head. No one paid him any attention, and at another time, in another life, this fact would have bothered him.

He smiled, feeling his cheeks wrinkle back. His face was too big, but that was all right; his friends in the tribe told him he would grow into it.

He walked over to a nearby trash can, reached into his back pocket, and pulled out his wallet. He thumbed through until he found his old ID and looked at the smiling face of a young man who would never again know the force of his father's fist.

Gregory Doe tossed the ID into the trash, grimacing as his muscles ached. The other Nobodies on the bus told him aspirin would be his best bet until he got used to his new skin.

A breeze blew past him, filling his nostrils with the scent of the salty Pacific, and he thought of Tommy. Tommy Keegan, with his sun-bleached hair. A fluttering ache rose up within his chest, and he frowned.

The other Nobodies didn't have a remedy for that. Heartache was something he couldn't shed, something he couldn't throw away. Can anyone?

'Them Iron Eyes Cody Blues'

by John Boden

Temple stabbed his walking stick into the scorched earth. It wept and gave purchase to the staff.

Groaning, he knelt by the river. It used to float free and wild. A liquid snake that seethed and hissed. Now its fetid waters congealed with poisons and monsters. The shoreline glistened with beads of mercury and caused the dead fish and bottles that bobbed there to shimmer in the dull sunlight. Once in a while, a slick tentacle or pincer claw would break the syrupy surface to pick at the floating dead. Bobbing near the water's edge was a large white lily.

He reached for the lily cluster and smiled. His eyes watered as he tried to capture the most beautiful thing he had seen since society shit the bed. The tears may have been from the fumes as well. His numb fingers grazed the syrupy current and grabbed the petals. The slimy bottom felt like phlegm or sludge. He lifted it to his watering eyes and lowered the surgical mask. It wasn't a lily. It was rotted head of cabbage. Its yellowed surface teaming with insects, wriggling and struggling to stay above the water level. He dipped it into the glowing swirls of water and shook the droplets free. They splattered the caked mud of the beach like blood spray. He pulled the mask away again and took a bite of the rotten vegetable. Thick ooze squirted from the sides as his brittle teeth tore into the addled meat of the heart. He belched and gagged but willed it down. His stomach so empty it literally sounded like someone dropped a rock in a dried up well. He held his jaw firm, allowing the vomit and acid to rise, tickle the back of his teeth and then recede. Pink snot began to trickle from his nose. He closed swollen eyes and smiled. In his mind, it was a fresh apple from his grandfather's orchard. He was basking in the warm sunlight as the sweet juice glazed his chin. Addy coughed and jarred Temple back to their festering reality.

Addy stood to the side. The smoky breeze fondled his greasy hair. He sighed, as he watched Temple eat the cabbage. "No ships, no sealing wax," Addy spoke. His voice a skull splitting under rock. A fly landed on his ear and crawled inside. Addy never flinched.

"So hungry, I'd have eaten Kings." Temple countered and spat at his feet. He rose to his staggering full height and took up his blackened walking stick. Addy raised his, which has a white flag on it. The flag was made from one of his old dress shirts from when he was a teacher, and they walked. Mirroring the banks of the slug that was a river that was once a snake.

* * *

They walked for miles and days and hours and months, all in a single afternoon. The cities were groaning carcasses, tilted buildings and nests of chain link and glass. Rubber tires and rat skeletons. Everything swarming with insects in children's clothes. There endless chittering and cries of "Food! Hungry!" were nails in their ears. They saw a little girl eating a dog, a dog that had been long dead. They saw a boy suckling from a goat. Its swollen udders leaking putrid milk down his eager face, its stillborn kid dangling from its hindquarters where it had stalled mid-delivery. The flies formed a buzzing cloak of privacy around them. Temple gagged and prayed. God ought to be used to bile-stained prayers. Addy stared at the ground and wept.

They kept walking. Kept bleeding beneath their makeshift

armor.

The fire was warm and lovely. Brilliant orange in contrast to the blackest black that was the night. The moon hung in the far corner, over the cliff cities. Its once white face now a bastard scowl caked with soot and tumor. Temple held his hands over the flames. His wedding ring was nearly invisible beneath the grime and crust. In the flicker, the sores wept like crying eyes. "What do you think will be there?" he asked Addy, "When we find The Untouched City."

Addy never moved. His arm across his exhausted eyes. The fire highlighting the bugs that toiled in his beard. Shimmering jewels in tangled brush. "Something." he answered, "Everything." He dozed and silence stomped into the camp, pissed on the fire and ordered them to bed. As Temple closed his eyes, he heard another mumbled word from his friend, "Nothing."

The night chopped the moon in two and each half slid into the land. The bloodstained clouds grumbled with growing thunder.

The two men slept and dreamed and in their dreams, they never awoke.

'Birdshirt'

by Troy Blackford

"I knew it once the birds hurt," he said, steepling his fingers and leering at me across the polished mahogany of his desk. At least, that's what it sounded like he said.

"Excuse me?"

His scowl deepened.

"Let me put this in terms you can understand, Mr. Pammelstock. My need to do this, of course, illustrates my point perfectly. You seem to be, at all times, working at the absolute limits of your comprehension around here."

I had to wonder if my boss, Chuck Crenshaw, calling me 'Pammelstock' was some kind of literary allusion. It certainly wasn't my name. I had no clue what he was talking about, and I got the feeling that's exactly how he wanted me to feel.

"Yes, absolutely pushed to the very limit of your comprehension," he said, nodding as if to demonstrate agreement with himself. "It really is quite horrifying."

"Horrifying?"

The man's choice of so strong a word made me even more uneasy than being called into his office. I had only been with the company for a few months, but, until this little chat began, I was under the impression that things had been going well. From the way my manager was talking to me now, I was forced to conclude they hadn't.

"Oh yes," Crenshaw said, continuing to nod while he pulled a stapler out of his upper desk drawer. "Completely horrifying. It's been called a limit—an absolute—by some scholars." He began to bang his fist down on the stapler, sending staples skittering across his desk.

I must have looked confused. But I felt beyond confused.

"Scholars," I began, achingly tentative, "have called my job performance 'an absolute?'"

I didn't believe this for a second, but I had to make sure I understood what I was hearing.

"Oh, you vainglorious detective, you. You think you know everything."

"I'm just trying to get clear on what you're saying."

"Yeah, well," he said, continuing to mash the stapler. A small flock of staples covered his desk like sunning gulls on a beach. "We keep circling around this one point, don't we?"

"The point of my comprehension?"

"Bingo!" he cried out with such sudden fervor that I juddered in my chair with alarm. "The exceptional proof within the pudding! You have nailed it down there, buddy. That's the bingo I was looking for."

I toyed with the idea of sliding my phone out of my pocket, just far enough to let me record the man's breakdown. I wanted to be able to prove my manager had lost it, in case this went to HR. I wasn't about to let an insane person determine the fate of my career. The staples now expended, however, Crenshaw refocused his eyes on me. I felt like a bug speared on an eagle talon. Way too freaked to try anything with my phone.

"I don't like bugs, Mr. Pepperdine," he said, slipping a blank index card out of a drawer and using it to shuffle the staples on his desk around into a neat pile.

"Excuse me?"

"You mentioned bugs just now, please. I don't like them."

"I don't recall saying anything about—"

He waved a hand dismissively.

"Yeah, yeah. But you looked like one. And I didn't like it."

"Well," I said, becoming braver in the face of his obvious instability. "You *looked* at me as though I were a bug."

"And what would you *like* to be when I look at you?"

I had no answer for that.

"Fact of the matter, Mr. Piperidine, you are in supreme trouble. You understand? Excessive, extreme troubles are coming your way. Troubles emblematic of your particular brand of misapprehension. What do you think of that?"

"I frankly don't know what to think."

"I'm *so* not surprised, Pepperidge."

He slapped the index card onto the desk and began to scribble on it furiously with a hot pink highlighter. This done, he threw the highlighter over his shoulder, where it struck his mirror and fell to the floor. He snapped the card up in his hand with a flourish and held it to his temple.

"You can redeem yourself completely, Mr. Popplestop, if you can do for me this singular favor, por favor."

"Namely?"

"'*Namely.*' I like that. It is baldly put. I will have to use this expression presently. But," he said, flailing an arm to wave away the digression, "the willing favor I need from you is this. I would very much find it agreeable if you could take a guess as to the identity of the graphemetic features I have inscribed on this planar surface. Can you do this for me?" His eyes shone with a sort of eager yet ravenous hunger, like a puppy addicted to heroin.

"You want me to tell you what you've written on there?" I asked.

"*Double* bingo!" he cried. He actually began to stomp his foot with glee. The gesture struck me as being something a drunk pirate would do when the pub's accordion player starts up their favorite song.

I bit my lip. I didn't have any way of guessing what the increasingly out-of-touch Crenshaw had written. I didn't really care. What's more, I felt more and more in danger as our little chat progressed. I was no longer worried about documenting the man's breakdown: clearly, he was past the point where convincing others he was fine would be possible. It wasn't my job I was worried about by this point, but my neck.

Still, it was probably best to humor him. I gave guessing my best shot. The man was clearly crazy, so it was probably something crazy.

"Bill Stickers whickers away the hours planting flowers?"

He looked at me, eyes agog. His lips flapped, like he was reading something difficult. His brows gyrated up and down, and as he squinted at me his tongue wriggled in the corner of his mouth, a fat pink worm shooting out between his lips.

He stared at me with such a peculiar expression that a wild, screeching part of my mind began to chant '*You guessed it! That's what he wrote!*' Crenshaw continued glaring at me as though I had just produced an uncooked hotdog out of my mouth.

"Well," I said after an uncomfortably spun-out silence, wanting his wild eyes off me. "Do I win the fair day goose?"

"You are a very *strange* young man," he said, slapping the card face down on his desk. "I want you to know that. Truly. The things that come out of your mouth are just... *Wow.*" He reached into his desk and pulled out a letter opener. It was the fanciest I had ever seen, with intricate scrolling woven all over the handle. "I have to wonder if you haven't begun to lose your mind, Mr. Picklepear. I really have to wonder."

"Can't be right every time," I said emptily, staring at the too-sharp-for-its-job tip of the letter opener as Crenshaw danced the point around with flourishes of his hand every bit as intricate as the scrolling on the thing's handle.

"No, absolutely not." He looked at me with a look of disdain I'd only ever seen from waiters in fancy restaurants. "*Of course* not."

He flipped the card over. I gasped.

"Bill Stickers whickers away the hours planting mulberries."

"A little joke," he said, producing another card.

This card, the actual first card, read "Bet you don't even see me write the next one."

I blinked at him.

"You were staring at the letter opener," he said, smiling broadly, obviously pleased with himself. He hoisted a second pink highlighter and flung this one over his shoulder, as well. It, too, skittered off the mirror. "Old Army trick."

"So you wrote down my guess while I—"

"Yes, yes," he said, waving me to silence once more. "We established that. My *word*, but you do seem to have the most incredible difficulties keeping up."

I took a deep breath and realized he was right, in a way. I'd let myself be distracted, all right. And in a much broader sense than the one Crenshaw meant.

I had to put an end to this little game. The only safe thing to do in this situation was to get up, get out of there, and alert... somebody. Tell the front desk. Call an ambulance. Transfer authority of the situation over to, well, the authorities.

I had let Crenshaw's babble lull me. The letter opener produced the opposite effect. Time to move.

"So," I said in a falsely cheerful voice, "am I free to go?"

"You know," he said in a thoughtful voice, rubbing the stubble on his chin with his free hand, "that's what I thought too. At least, until I saw the birdshirt."

"The birdshirt?"

"*Seriously?*" he bellowed. "That was one of the *very first things I said* to you when you came in here. Mr. Pidgeonpickle, you have *slipped*. Slipped right off your cracker."

I knew he was talking nonsense, but I still stopped and racked my brain in an attempt to remember if this was true. Then it hit me.

"'I knew it once the *birdshirt!*'" I blurted aloud. He hadn't said 'once the birds hurt,' but 'birdshirt.'

"What on *earth* are you saying?"

"That's what *you* said! You said 'I knew it once the birdshirt.'"

He shook his head. "Such a promising young man, too."

"It is!" I implored. "You said exactly that."

"Well, bra-*fuckin'*-vo, buddy," he said, his tone abruptly changing. "You remember *some* of what I said." He set the letter opener down and began a slow clap. "I'll put you in for the coveted 'Still a Total Dumbass Award.'"

My curiosity helped me to ignore the affront to my intelligence, along with the stinging fact that I truly *was* stupid to remain in Crenshaw's office.

"What's a bird shirt?" I asked.

He leaned back in his chair, stared up at the ceiling, and sighed, his arms limp at his sides.

"*Arrrrrrgh!*" he moaned, lurching abruptly across the desk and stamping his feet like a child having a tantrum.

I watched with detached fascination as he picked up his letter opener, placed it between his two palms, and began to rapidly spin it, drilling into the expansive mahogany desk like a boy scout trying to start a campfire.

"Namely, the bird shirt is where the words hurt. The bird shirt makes the flowers turn into mulberries."

I didn't think I had made the right decision. I should have left when I had the chance.

"Well, it's been nice chatting with you," I said, pushing the chair away from the desk and rising.

"No, it hasn't," Crenshaw said, his voice blank. His eyes gleamed at the sawdust his letter opener was kicking up.

I moved towards the door, biting my lip and hoping he wouldn't say or do anything else. My fingers touched the cold metal of the knob when he spoke.

"Wait!" he cried.

Nevertheless, my fingers turned.

"Don't go out there!" He sounded scared.

I, against all better judgment, instinctively turned to look at him.

"There's wolves out there!" he said, his eyes wide and his jaw slack. He began to chip away at the pit he had carved into his desk, stabbing the letter opener into the depression as though it were an ice pick.

"I'll take my chances," I said.

"Yeah, well: so will the wolves," he said, turning his attention back to the desk.

I stepped out, closed the door, and leaned against it. I took a deep breath. And, I admit, for a second I *did* look quickly down the hallway in both directions, straining my ears for the soft scuffle of padded feet, the gently clinking *tink, tink, tink* of claws clacking quietly on tile.

'Various Other Modalities'

by Val Tenterhosen

Breathing is what the Lord designated me to do. He gave me two pink lungs so I could go forth and inhale. I worked it all out on a giant placemat one night at Sal's diner over on Forty-Eight and Allegro. All I have to do is align my nose with one of seventy-five possible permutations. The key thing is that my philtrum be oriented to the various rotational axes of the Earthly magnetic fields. Piece of cake.

The Lord makes a point to let me in on profound little secrets like this one. The lessons come in a diverse array of modalities. Example: I made a perfect platter once but I dropped it. It took me three weeks to realize what *that* meant.

When I finally got the picture, it was like something clicked. When all that soul-searching finally pays off, you know you're bound for bigger and better things. Something special would soon come my way.

And wouldn't you know it, it did. It all came out in the end, all right. The Lord is mysterious, but never say there's something He can't do.

I was in the public restroom at the library down on Valejo and Honoria when it happened. I hadn't shaved in a few days, so I wanted to take care of that. Only cut myself three times. That, in itself, was a sort of sign.

Then, I moved on to that other business you take care of at the library. Not all that easy when you eat what I eat. But I managed to deal with the matter with resplendent ease, on this most special of days.

It was the Lord, working His way through me.

I thought to myself, 'You know, scout? That was too easy.' It had to mean something. I looked into the toilet bowl, scouring for clues, and that's when I saw it. A divine vision permitted by the grace of the Lord.

A perfectly formed shit seahorse swam merrily around, down inside the toilet bowl. His little brown eyes seemed to track me as he orbited the porcelain. As he made his tiny laps, his little curlicue tail bobbed in rhythm with his head.

He was perfect. I was speechless.

The Lord truly is righteous. I knew right then what He wanted me to do. I reached for the flush, and set the newest of all His creations loose; down into the drainpipes, out into the world, its time at last come.

'Holiday in Modal City'.

by M.C. O'Neill

I'm little again and find myself lost from my family among the towering trees. They're everywhere now and I can smell the stink of ragweed invading my nose, but for some reason, the back of my throat doesn't itch and I don't need to make barnyard noises to scratch out the tickle.

Direction means nothing anymore as the umber trunks surround me any which way I turn. For some reason, I'm not scared. I should be since I no longer have a clue where my parents are. Something about all of this is enjoyable, soothing, like I'm supposed to be here. *Yes*, I decide--*I'm supposed to be here*.

Greens and browns are punctuated with the intense, almost annoying colors of fruit, flora and buglife. Stunned by it all, my fugue is broken by a rustling from out of the undergrowth. She'll be here again today. She'll come out and play. It's so much more fun than a boring picnic with Mommy and Daddy.

Covered in the arboreal growth from which she emerged, the girl giggles as she twirls the long, scarlet hair from beneath the wreath swirled around her head. She looks like an all-natural little princess and I cannot say anything, not even "Hello," because her beauty seems to paralyze me. This is not a bad thing, though. She'll never hurt me because she is a princess of life. She makes me laugh.

"Play with me, Ankit." Her words wobble in a fog, like something sung from out of the aether. Just as her face is dazzling, her voice is beautiful and calms me like an infusion of Placix, but this is the real feeling. Natural. It's all-natural.

Ever graceful, she holds out an apple. A real, red one. Its hue is hyper-bright and it almost stings my eyes to look at it, but the pain subsides as fast as it had appeared. Without any sense of fear, I reach for her gift and her little brown fingers caress mine as I accept. She smiles.

I bite. I can't resist it. Flavors unknown to me invade my brain, like a kiss. I'm shocked by it all and she laughs. My happy face must look comical to her.

As always, while I chew, the fragrance of the fruit mushes and soon turns to foul rot in my mouth. The undergrowth bursts alive with a vile explosion and that monster makes its grand appearance once again.

Horrible, as always, the tiger roars with the strength of a hundred screams. Its battle-taunt reverberates in my skull. The beast is real, not a clone or a chimera. It has no inhibitions or inhibitors and it is not for exhibition. I want to fall asleep from terror and vomit from the taste of the offal sloshing in my mouth and the horror in my soul. I want to die.

She pierces the forest with a scream for help. So loud, she never stops, creating a relentless beat of alarm. As to her answer, the sky darkens and the forest begins to sprout mold... then it all *spoils* in the night. Everything spoils.

Still screaming, the tiger ignores my girl, my love, while I dribble the rank mush out of my frozen maw. Its eyes glow. It pounces, it strikes. It strikes at me.

* * *

The morning alarm's wail is deafening, as usual. I wish I was allowed a gun for once just so I can aim from under my blanket without looking and blow it away. Kill it.

"*Ankit Ganesh, arise!*" the harsh, female voice barks over the bleating pulse of the beep. "*It is time for work. Today is Monday, Twenty-one, April. Wake up! Work, work, work!*"

"Screw, screw you," I grumble, still hidden under my one blanket.

"Insubordination will not be tolerated, Ankit Ganesh." That brisk, grating voice has a semi-responsive AI and sounds like it was pre-recorded somewhere in the Nu-Brit Sector. "How would you like the Corporation to give you a demerit today? No, I should not think so. Remember, tardiness is not a value of the Flyborg Foods Corporation."

"I don't think you think about anything much more than how to annoy me," I argue, half-asleep, with my alarm clock.

"Humph," it responds in feigned bother. "Well, Ankit Ganesh, I am forced to commence your countdown. At its termination, a demerit will be preemptively sent to Flyborg HQ and duly recorded in your permanent..."

I growl and hop out of the cot in one movement. "All right! I'm awake! See?"

Dancing around in front of the Regulex unit, I make rude faces to the creepy, fleshy tyrant. I just want to fall back into bed and continue my sweet nightmare.

With its typical, condescending tone, it says, "Excellent. And remember, Ankit Ganesh, you are not allowed any sugar in your meal rations today."

"Why? Are you trying to call me fat, or something?"

She — well — *it*, tisks. "There are no fat citizens in Monotown, Ankit Ganesh, according to our last census cycle."

I roll my eyes to that. "Gee, I haven't noticed."

"I detect sarcasm in your vocal patterns, Ankit Ganesh. You will require a dose of Placix today."

Placix. More Placix today. Bouncing over to that horrible bio-fixture growing out of my wall with feigned joy, I press my lips to the pulpy half-orb installed in its middle and give it a wet kiss. "See, that's why you're so smart, Regulex."

"But of course!" she responds, failing to detect more of my rancor. "My central processor is currently operating at 7.1 terabytes with another upgrade scheduled for later this month. Next year, the U.S. Biotics Corporation is set to outfit me with a small laser-emitting polyp so that you and I can be more up-close and personal. And, to add to that, I will be…"

Ignoring her veiled threats, I trudge over nude to the powder shower and Regulex activates it while still attempting to scare me with her array of horrible, planned upgrades courtesy of this corporation and that corporation. Thus far, she really has no way to punish me other than to snitch to Flyborg HQ, but if she could ever dole out physical pain, such a thought gives me a momentary shudder. The last thing I need is for her to zap me in the rump with a laser just because I farted in my sleep.

Jets of disinfectant cloud the room as I wait in my impatience for the contraption to finish. Not only is my body being cleansed — the agent tingles — so is the entire dorm. It stinks of talcum, orange and peppermint.

Not much here to clean, really. Monomodals like me are only allotted one hundred fifty square feet for personal habitat.

Being a monomodal, it's not like I'll ever worry about sharing it with a wife as none of us are licensed to reproduce. Neither do the dimodals, but they get twelve extra square feet in their flats. Of course, their Regulexes are a wee bit larger.

The dust settles and Regulex jets the remaining powder off my body. Sometimes, I think this is the best part of my day. It's like hundreds of invisible fingers caressing me for thirty seconds. I wish it would last for at least an hour.

I strap on my tan jumpsuit and don my red smock, I check the tiny mirror affixed on the Medcab. Like always, I look like refried crap after having had one of those nightmares and I swipe off some forgotten powder out of my short, black hair.

"*Placix*, Ankit Ganesh! Remember, you are required to dose!" She barks like it's a sector-wide emergency.

Not even bothering to grumble, I open the Medcab and dig a pill out of the dispenser's rack. As always, it's fully stocked with my medical modifications.

I hate Placix. The dope is designed to bind with my body's pheromone production. It's sky-blue and is as big as a large man's thumb. Swallowing it dry is a chore, but there's really no way of getting around it as Corporate will know I've avoided my dose with their pheromone sensors at the gate. If they don't smell it on me, I get a demerit. *Time to get neutralized*, I think while navigating the horrid thing down my throat. It kind of tastes like sweat.

For some reason, I tell Regulex goodbye as I grab my plastic skullcap and goggles. I really hate that thing, but she almost serves as my only family. Maybe it's just the drugs taking effect, making me less randy, more agreeable.

A Monotown morning invades my dulling senses the instant I step out the door onto the tramway's balcony. Such boisterous chaos makes me grateful for the Placix just so I can zone out while waiting for the Loop Liner.

"City Crack — East Sector! Monotown City Crack!" A pentamodal is buzzing some nosey-parker warning to a superior through the comm in his helmet. He sounds more like a bot than Regulex, but there is a real person buried somewhere underneath all of that bulky, orange gear. It's the first sound my ears are assaulted with as I step outside.

Of course, everybody calls the pentamodals simply "The Five." Most of we monomodals refer to them as "bulls," and that they are. Any monomodal with their wits about them would give those bullies a wide berth.

Another Fiver driving a flycle lands on the wide balcony, apparently in response to the frantic bull's electronic whinging. The cop dismounts and assists his comrade in surrounding a diminutive woman done up in her daily work gear. It's of the same cut and design as mine, but adorned in the colors of the Burger Punk Corporation, our competitor. She's a monomodal too. Everyone living on this block of my city crack is one.

Out of one ear, I attempt to listen in to what the commotion is all about, but my medmods blend together the sounds of the city's bustle. Makes it difficult to focus my curiosity.

"She had red hair," the woman explains to the bull. "I saw it coming out from under her skullcap."

Red hair? Nobody in these parts has red hair, not unless they are of the higher castes and can afford to dye it. Definitely not monomodals. It's apparent the Burger Punk woman is not in trouble, but rather, snitching on someone.

The Fivers buzz and wheeze at her and their tone soon ramps to anger. Despite her offer to help them, it backfires. Within moments, they render her in a position of arrest and cuff her wrists with twisties. She howls, "No!" but her pleas are worthless.

Everyone in Monotown knows never to talk to the Five. Not even to help them and definitely not to ask for assistance. Any monomodal who even looks a Five in the eye runs the great risk of being taken away. *Silly Burger Punk*, I think.

At last, the damn Loop Liner arrives. An immense monopole nightmare, the behemoth halts under its overtrack and swishes it doors open. This Liner services the floor of my block's balcony as well as the levels two above and three below.

I board it and grab an available hanger as quick as possible. The Monotown Loop Liner is standing-room-only. Thousands of monomodals pack into the cabin's belly six levels deep for a day of labor. Gods, how I hate this thing.

Per usual, Samarkand Ganesh – no relation – files onto the hanger behind me. Another Flyborg employee, Samar is one of the closest people whom I can consider a friend. We both work in the Protein Processing Department.

"Oi, you see that Burger Punk minger get what-for down the balco, Kit?" Samar whispers over my shoulder.

I nod. "Aye, mate. Never gob it with a Fiver, yeah? Fat bastards."

"Too right. It takes a corpee emergency to muster those wobbles, innit?"

"Too right," I agree. "Wonder what that one was going on about?"

He huffs. "Who knows? Snitches dig ditches and all that. Serves her right, if you ask me."

"Dunno," I shrug. "Might have been a solid reason."

Samar chuckles to that. "No, mate. Ain't no good reason to converse with the Five."

He coughs and excuses. "Oi, Kit. Reggie got you on dope today? You're slow."

"Yeah, the slag munted me up," I confess.

"You on the Six, innit?" he prods.

I nod to that. "Yeah, Placix, of course. It's already in effect."

He leans in closer behind me. "Aye, on that topic, I got a hold of some Dromeda for the corpee rave this weekend. Flyborg's actually gonna let us monos in for this one. Samar's gonna go galactic!"

"Shh!" I hiss. "Don't let the whole Liner know. Where in the hells did you cop that kind of gear anyway? You know only High Modals are allowed it."

"I so happen to have my leads." He pounds his sunken chest with pride. "And, I've got enough for the 'gither of us. So, don't say I never did you right."

"Heh, it's probably pish," I joke, but only halfway. No mono could ever hope to score Dromeda.

"You won't say that whilst in orbit, son."

"Sure," I whisper. "But what if I..."

Our banter is interrupted by the blaring beep-beep-beep of

the Loop Liner's PSA screen affixed at the front of our cabin. Modal City demands our attention once again, like it does almost every morning. We shut our mouths and concede to the screen's wishes.

Attention Citizens of Modal City!

Crime report for Twenty-one, April:

Monotown: City Crack – East Sector.

"The body of dimodal citizen Ankit Patel of the Berenjee Diamond Corporation has been found this morning outside of Cistern 200 of this community's sewer system. Pentamodal officials report that the only trauma to the body found was a series of multiple puncture marks caused by what appear to be thorns of an unknown origin. Although a blood analysis and autopsy has yet to be conducted, poison is a presumed agent in his death.

"Citizens of Monotown are expected to stop, look and listen for any suspicious activity as this assailant is still at large. As Patel's body was found semi-nude, it is assumed the assailant had stolen the victim's clothing. If you have any information regarding this crime, please report your findings to the Pentamodal substation of your city crack.

"Thank you for your cooperation."

"Oi!" Samar cheers. "The poor bastard's name is Ankit! You're dead, mate."

"I'm no Patel and I'm certainly no dimodal." I shrug off Samar's jest. "Besides, what do I know about processing diamonds?"

Peering out the window, I grow bored with my mate's

humor and attempt to soak in the view of Modal City. The windows are so small on the Loop Liner, just tiny round portholes. I muse for an instant how it always seems like I am inside and can never catch a good view of anywhere.

My flat has only one porthole on the door, not much bigger than the ones on the Liner and there are no windows at all to be found at work, at least not in my department. To think of it, the only times I can enjoy fresh air is out on the balcony before and after work. One day, I suspect the city will enclose these as well. Modal City always grows like that. Terrible.

There really isn't anything worth looking at anyway, except the sun. After the Green Flu had wilted all plant life on Earth — *all* of it — there is now only the dirge of Modal City for the eyes to enjoy. Word on the wire is, beyond her walls, there is nothing but wastes, and as such, it's Modal City or death.

It had happened almost overnight, that Green Flu. Despite all the dope Regulex pumps into my brain, I still remember trees and plants and fruits and all the rest of it quite well. Sure, we have fruits and vegetables, but they are manufactured out of various DNA combinations and packaged as a goopy paste.

Truth be told, it all tastes disgusting and no matter how many happy little cartoons Corporate slaps on their plastic tubes, none of it will ever be like crunching into a real apple. I miss apples so much.

We travel on in vapid bliss, and before I can get used to it, the Liner slows and halts. It's time for another day, just like the one before it.

The gates of the Flyborg Foods Corporation stand beyond the balcony. This isn't the only gate, of course. Levels above and levels below, those balconies host their own gates where hundreds upon hundreds of monomodals like me file inside the bulk of the monolithic structure. Once again, I have a brief enjoyment of life *outside*. I love and hate being outside because I know this experience is fleeting and nothing more than a fluke in the grid. Yes, the city will seal this over some day, I'm certain of it.

We all queue and wait for each worker to pass the gate's inspection. Bio-polyps and carbuncles scan and sensor every one of us to make certain that, 1) we're not corporate spies and, 2) we are complying with our medmod prescriptions for the day.

It's my turn for inspection and a fleshy appendage swings down, grabs my face and claws my eyes wide open. It stinks of eggs. A brief flash to the brain and I get dizzy for a second. From somewhere I can never seem to identify, a humanlike voice buzzes.

"Monomodal #2275 - Ganesh, Ankit," it hisses. *"Employment status: Pass. Modification compliance: Pass. Please enter for work."*

"Go die," I grumble to the bio-monster in defiance and comply with its request. I don't worry any as this thing is too stupid to take offense to my insubordinate epithets, unlike Regulex.

Ambling forth, my workbench awaits. The Protein Processing Department of the Flyborg Foods Corp is all I ever see of this place. We monomodals aren't allowed beyond this facility. It's really nothing more than an enormous floor segmented into countless sections of an identical kind. Efficient, yes, but designed for the lowest of the low — us. There is nothing more bottommost than a monomodal.

We work alongside the dimodals, but they have more

"esteem," or rather, work-value than us. Mostly unskilled maintenance, dimodals are allowed to boss us around to an extent. As for esteem, Regulex can sense if we have too much of it for our place in life. That's why she drugged me today, because I showed too much backbone. *"Processors can't expect to be designers,"* she scolds me on a regular basis.

As for processing, my first chimera for the day plops down in front of me from a portal in the ceiling the moment I arrive to my station. Since much of the animal life on Earth perished along with the plants during the Green Flu, Flyborg and other horrible corporations like Burger Punk bio-engineer their own livestock out of rogue DNA. The result is a hodgepodge beast of multiple genetic origins designed to yield the most meat for the smallest cost.

My job is to yank out assholes. There is no better way to describe it. The thing in front of me today is an enormous hybrid lobster mixed with a sheep - a wooly lobster. I've never seen anything like it before, but each day, the bastards up in Genetics treat us with a new monster to prepare. Some days, I swear to Shiva my subjects are part human being. Most days, I pray Shiva would just wash this all away.

Grabbing its flat tail, I lift it up and search through the fleece for my target. It's so disgusting. With any kind of sea life, it's difficult for me to pinpoint its anus, but this thing is a bio-labyrinth. At last, I find the thing's butthole. It's a sheep's sphincter, so this one will be a bit easier to excise. I pick up my paring knife and commence my horrid labor.

"Trimodal on the floor!" our floorman, Aarpit Bhoola wails as he rushes in. "Trimodal on the floor!"

Bhoola is minor management. We all hate him, of course, even the brownnosers. The best thing about Bhoola is his irritable bowel. *Pure comedy.*

A bit thicker than we monos, Aarpit enjoys more calories than us. Whatever the higher-ups are feeding him isn't good for his digestion.

Squatting for a moment, our manager emits a concussive blast out of his rectum. It's apparent he does this in thinking that it asserts his authority and I bite down on my tongue to belay laughter.

"Labor report, Twenty-one, April!" he hollers. He farts again. A fellow mono can't contain her gaiety and snickers.

"Shut up, you motherfucker!" Bhoola reprimands the unknown joker at top volume. This only leads to half of the floor cracking up; I'm no exception despite my morning doping.

Brushing it off, Bhoola clears his throat and grabs the suspended floor-mic. "Today, you buttholes will be processing what the people up in Genetics call 'lobzillas.' As you can see before you, it is a new breed of animal. Seafood and wool all-in-one. I want you morons in meat processing to shuck them and I want you morons in hide processing to fleece them. Is that so hard for you shitheads to understand?"

"No, Armpit!" We respond in unison, muxing his name on purpose, like always.

"Good," he spits. "Now it is time to sing the *Flyborg Corporate Anthem.*"

An electronic jingle bursts over the P.A. at once and we commence belting out the stupid song after four bars:

"All hail Flyborg!

Flyborg great and grand!

Keeps us modals safe and warm,

From the dangers of the Wasteland.

Work hard daily, stay sharp too,

Show up one and all!

If you fail too many times,

We'll boot you over the wall!"

Bhoola grunts, disgusted. "All right, get to work, you nincompoops!" With that, he about-faces, squats and farts right into the mic just to pack in his spite for us. Uproarious laughter from the floor follows, to which he storms off and flashes us a rude gesture before disappearing away to a place unknown.

I continue the day performing my dreadful duties in my drugged stupor. My brain is half switched off and I'm thankful for that because digging into a frankenmonster's bowels is nothing short of disgusting, no matter the rubber gloves.

I'm fed a tube of food paste at brunch, lunch, tea and dinner — all four meals taste like pure crap. Monomodals must dine at work every day, as our flats are too small to accommodate a kitchen. Corporate wants us to eat nothing but Flyborg food anyway, so we are dependent on it regardless of how foul it tastes.

After enjoying the evening gloom on the balcony for a few minutes, I hop the Loop Liner and try to keep from nodding off while standing. Once again, the screen at the front of the cabin alerts us to the murder of that dimodal, though no breaking developments have arisen since this morning.

Regulex begins harping on me the instant I return home. Her prattle thunders on before I have even closed my door. "Ankit Ganesh! Welcome back. It is now time for your nightly dose of Somex."

"Mind if I get a wee bit comfy first?" I argue with the monstrosity in my wall.

"Somex is all the comfort you'll need for tonight, Ankit Ganesh," she retorts. "Report to your Medcab and prepare to administer."

Skag, I sneer to myself. I hate Regulex. Anyone in their right mind hates her too. Dope and threats—that's really her only functions. That and snitching.

Somex is the worst drug ever designed by the Von Bump Corporation (GmbH). If it couldn't get any worse, the thing is about half the size of my fist. It is, to be honest, just another frankenmonster in the form an enormous pill.

I wander over to the Medcab and grab the beast-drug. Much like a fleshy grub, the thing squeals and writhes within my grip. Placix may taste like sweat, but Somex tastes like shit. Closing my eyes, I open my mouth and let the dope do its work.

Since we are not allowed water in our flats, Somex was engineered to crawl down our throats to assist in digestion despite its bulk. It slithers in my gullet and I want to die. I can feel the anomaly wriggling into my system. Still clothed, I hop in my cot and let the little monster do its job.

"Sweet dreams, Ankit Ganesh," Regulex taunts in her

spiteful treacle.

"I hope you reincarnate into a lobzilla," I mumble; my brain is already fogged. I'll be knocked out for the next twelve hours.

* * *

Again, the forest surrounds me. I'm bathed in unearthly starshine and it illuminates what's left of my spirit. Sights, sounds and aromas I've not known since childhood invade my brain. It's so good to be here and I never want to leave this beautiful night.

I can't talk, I can't think. I look down at my nudity and see that I'm—and this is certain—not a child. Listening to the chorus of life around me, I await to hear her arrive. Just for me, like every night.

Brambles rustle and she appears out of the roiling nature, like always. It's my girl. Her body is festooned in flowers not long forgotten by man. Hibiscus, roses, chrysanthemums; all of them swirl about her umber skin. Like me, she's mature now. Her hips are thick and tiny fruits of which I've never known cover her plump breasts like a natural brassiere.

"Ankit," she moans. It's a supernatural call and her plush lips don't even move. She calls to me and her mind is like music.

Paralyzed, I wait for her nightly apple. Her hands are empty, however. Both of them reach out for me and I feel a pang of dread for a second. I want to be sick.

Her fragrance assaults me and I love it. It isn't the phony stenches manufactured by the corporations. It's so real that it's much like time travelling back to my childhood days when there was true life all around me.

Tonight, we will not share a meal. My girl invades my senses with an alien odor that stiffens me. Gyrating in a slight, seductive dance, she stretches her arms behind her crimson mane and exposes clusters of violets and leaves sprouting out of her flesh hither and yon. Her fragrance makes my heart race.

Time jumps and she is upon me. I can't seem to understand how she got this close, yet here we are.

At first, she's so soft, and this belies her wiry physique. Without realizing it, I'm on my back and she is atop me. Her perfumes become more intense with every moment and I love it. Never would I think this could happen to a monomodal like me.

These tender embraces become savage as the night wears on. Her skin hardens and more flora blooms about her with each of her movements. Her face begins to match her ferocity, but it isn't an angry energy and I feel no fear amidst my lust.

I'm entangled. I can't move as I've become literally rooted. Vines, thorns and bramble constrict my limbs and dig into my skin. I'm bleeding, but her sap kills the pain. Soon, I feel full in an odd way; like I've just finished a grand meal unlike I've ever eaten.

My flesh has become a part of her as I see that I too am budding. My tan skin is browning and fibers run through it like so much xylem and phloem. She is lost to my sight amongst our entwined foliage, but I can feel her regardless.

As a child, I had always called her "Apple," but now I know her true name: *Malini*. It's a special secret that only I have the privilege of knowing.

"What about the tiger? The beast?" I warn to her with my mind.

Her toxins soothe any of my fears. "There is no tiger here. I've taken care of him. He is no longer our concern."

Closing my eyes, I let the light of the stars warm my lids and enjoy my journey into her. There will be no tiger tonight.

* * *

"Ankit Ganesh! You have... Ankit... Reboot permission failure. Track seventeen... Jack be nimble... No comply... Tripped over the candlestick. Fish... Trench... HELP!"

Regulex's frightened blathering wakes me. I'm so confused. Eyes open, I need to understand what lies before me. Everything is so strange this morning.

Leaves and vines writhe everywhere. It's as if I'm in a nursery. Life dances and hovers around me. Flowers, fronds, fruit and moss create a symphony of natural wonder and confusion. I haven't seen this since I was a little boy. The tiny ray of light from my round porthole promises me it's morning, but one like no other.

I open my mouth and vomit pollen. It's difficult to speak and it's hard to breathe.

She sits astride Regulex's top shelf and swings her feet like a little girl in the throes of boredom. *It's her!* Malini. Her long, brown legs amble back and forth and her breasts bleed amber syrup. Red hair, just as I remember, blows wild in an airless atmosphere. Her florid body odor sweetens the entire place. A discarded Berenjee Diamond Corp uniform is rumpled on the ground amidst a bed of bramble.

"Good morning, Ankit," she giggles. "We have such great things ahead of us today!"

I belch out more hay fever in response. This isn't insubordination, just a natural reaction. An ancient reaction. I try to arrest it with my throat muscles.

"Stop it, Malini!" I choke amongst the leaves. "Never sit on Regulex! She'll have us killed! Booted over the wall!"

"No," she saunters over to me and is now soothing my cheek. "That won't happen. Regulex is gone now. She cannot hurt us. She cannot destroy our love. I've made her blind and stupid."

"No! I must be at work today!" I argue. "I must report every day!"

"You are wrong, my little seed." She caresses my chin. It's bearded with moss "You have a new job now. Your corporations mean nothing, love. We can play all day!"

At that suggestion, my attempt to move my arms is arrested by the piercing ache through my muscles. With each second of effort, my body is stiffening. In the morning gloom of the porthole, I can see that my skin is turning to bark. The foliage around me is, in truth, coming out of me.

The flowers and fronds of my dreams are now a waking reality. I am blooming by the minute.

More pollen and seeds blow out of my mouth as I try to continue my protest. My throat is clogged with the stuff and I don't know how I am going to breathe.

Malini embraces me and I have no ability to return the gesture. I'm paralyzed. Regulex continues her pathetic cries for help and her language becomes all the more nonsensical.

"We can play forever," Malini whispers into my ear.

* * *

Breaking News!

Monotown: City Crack - East Sector.

Tuesday. Twenty-two, April.

"Pentamodal officials are reporting what appears to be a large tree growing out of the Monotown address of monomodal citizen Ankit Ganesh, an employee of the Flyborg Foods Corporation. The exact nature of this growth is unknown as of yet, and Septimodal officials are currently preparing an investigation of this strange phenomenon, as the tree had appeared seemingly overnight.

"If this is indeed a tree, it will prove to be the first of its kind since the Green Flu had destroyed all plant life on Earth almost fifteen years ago. Could this incident mark the return of natural vegetation to the planet? Only time and investigation will tell. We will inform you of any breaking news regarding this situation as we learn more about it.

"Pentamodal officials are searching for Ankit Ganesh, as his whereabouts are currently unknown. Officials are withholding a lead on a possible connection between Ganesh and the dimodal found murdered near his city crack yesterday morning. Any information leading to Ganesh's location or relation to this phenomenon must be reported to your local Pentamodal substation.

"In other news, an explosion at the Burger Punk Corporation killed nearly two hundred monomodal and dimodal

employees in their Protein Processing Department.
Septimodal inspectors blame the explosion on faulty wiring
in an out-of-date scrubber."

'Zonkey'

by Tom Bordonaro

"Hey, Chris! Whaddya know, paisan?" Charlie behind the bar yells after the bell above the door goes ding-ding and Christopher Columbus walks into the joint.

The two other regulars look up, squinting at the bright morning light that has come in behind Chris. The daylight decides this ain't its kinda place and slides quickly back outside as the door swings closed.

"Christopher," Morrie says and gives a little wave before going back to his beer. Morrie is wearing his blue sweater today. His hair is curly and grey.

A couple of stools down, Ring-A-Ding Lawrence is still squinting at the hastily departed daylight. Years of church-basement boxing matches have punched some of the gears out of his internal clock.

"Morrie. Larry. Charlie," Chris says, taking a seat. He removes his hat and hands it to Charlie, who puts it behind the bar. Chris' hat has a feather in it and Ring-A-Ding Lawrence often confuses it for a chicken. Ring-A-Ding may not be able to tell the difference between a hat and a chicken, but he knows that a chicken does not belong in a tavern. Charlie started hiding it after Chris got tired of retrieving it off of the sidewalk. Charlie figures it's the least he can do. The guy did discover America, after all.

"The usual for you," Charlie says to Chris, flipping his dishcloth over one shoulder and clinking a few ice cubes into a glass. "How 'bout you, Angelo?"

Angelo, perched on Christopher Columbus' right shoulder, stretches his tiny wings and looks over the rows and glorious rows of beautiful booze behind Charlie, trying to decide. Unlike Chris, Angelo leaves his hat on. It helps Ring-A-Ding tell the difference between Angelo and a parakeet which, according to Ring-A-Ding, has even less place in a tavern than a chicken. No stranger to the sidewalk himself, Angelo just leaves the pull tab-sized halo where it is.

Angelo rubs his tiny hands together and stares, mesmerized by the army of bottles in formation under the neon beer signs and long mirror. He feels like a commanding general in review of the troops, deciding which soldier is the most fit for a very special mission. In this case, to get him wasted out of his skull.

"Oh man," Angelo says, mostly to himself, "Fuck yeah. Holy fucking shit, yeah."

Charlie puts Chris' drink, a White Russian, in front of him, "I thought that other one had the foul mouth," he says, pointing to Chris' empty left shoulder, "He off today?"

Chris sips his drink, "Stan? Naw, he had to murder a busload of nuns and orphans."

"You don't say?"

"Well, he's a devil. It's what they do," Chris says and shrugs. When he does, Angelo falls over and lands in the poofy sleeve thing on Chris' shoulder. Shaken out of his fascination, Angelo reminds himself to get Chris to start shopping at the Gap, maybe get some khakis. The velvet and leggings get up is centuries out of style. Plus, it makes the guy look like a faggot.

"So?" Charlie says.

66

"I'll have a Zonkey," Angelo says.

Charlie rolls his eyes, "Does this look like the kind of place that serves those fairy drinks? No offense."

"Hey!" Angelo says, pointing a wee finger, "I'm a seraphim, not a fairy. You wanna watch that smart mouth on you."

"Yeah, yeah. Go on," Charlie says, not bothered at all. He's been a bartender for years and knows that some guys are real touchy. Especially the little ones.

"Angelo, take it easy," Chris says.

"Hey! He asked me what I wanted and I told him. Now he don't wanna make it. Plus he wants to be a wise guy."

"Hello Christopher Columbus!" Ring-A-Ding Lawrence yells from his end of the bar. Chris, sipping his drink, flips a hand in greeting.

Angelo scowls in the old heavyweight's direction, "Cock-a-doodle-doo, retard. Rise and shine! We've been here for like an hour and a half already!"

"Angelo, take it easy," Chris says calmly.

Charlie puts his hands out, palms forward, "Hey, look. I said no offense. Tell you what, you tell me how to make your drink and I'll make your drink."

Angelo rubs his tiny chin, "Shit. I was hoping you'd know. I mean, you're the fucking bartender, right? Supposed to know how to make drinks and shit. I could understand I ask you to do algebra. But c'mon..."

"Mayhap I can be of some assistance?" says the horse sitting to their left. Actually, it doesn't look like a horse. It looks like a mule with stripes.

Chris, Angelo, and Charlie blink. Double takes all around. No one heard this thing come in. Morrie gives a little wave and goes back to his beer.

"What the fuck?" Angelo says.

"We didn't hear you come in," Chris explains.

"No bell," Charlie adds, and points to the bell over the door.

The horse laughs politely, "Ah, yes. Most sorry about that. Studied the ancient art of ninjitsu for some time in the Orient. Traipsing about unseen and unheard, assassinating samurais and all that blather. Still have a penchant for skulking around. Force of habit, really. So sorry."

Angelo says, "Wait a minute... you're French?" It is more of an accusation.

"That's a British accent, Angelo," Chris says and nods at the horse for confirmation.

"Quite right, old bean. From Brixton, originally."

"A British horse," Angelo says, and then adds, "Great," apropos of nothing.

"A Zonkey, actually," the Zonkey says. "You see, my mother was a donkey and my paterfamilias was a zebra. Now, I don't mean to intrude, but I understand that you've been having a spot of bother with the formulation of a specific libation?"

Charlie looks at Chris who looks at Angelo who is glowering at the Zonkey.

Angelo slowly says, "What?"

"Hello horsey!" From Ring-A-Ding's end of the bar.

"The drink," the Zonkey explains, "You ordered a libation colloquially known as a 'Zonkey' from the publican here who expressed an inability to make said potation for lack of knowledge of the proper ingredients.

"A most common occurrence these days, actually, what with there being a plethora of different appellations for any given singular alcoholic concoction. Now, when I was the head bartender at the Ritz during the early Twenties and I invented the Manhattan, people all across the world called it just so. 'May I have a Manhattan, please?' they would say from Borneo to Bangkok Bay and all points in between.

"Even the delightful F. Scott Fitzgerald, who had a flair for the written word, as you know, referred to this marvelous drink as a Manhattan. 'Zonkey,' F. Scott would say, 'I have given much thought to that drink of yours known as a Manhattan. While I find the name a bit tired and uninspiring, I must admit that it fits this particular liquid refreshment and is quite utilitarian. It is as easy to remember as the wonderful city in which it was first created! Therefore, instead of trying to come up with a different name, I will just refer to it as a Manhattan. And I will have five of them, if you please'.

"Sadly, that was anon. No point living in the past, say I! So, on with the matter at hand. You will all be happy to know that the appurtenance and constituents for this particular libation are relatively simplistic in nature. First, you start with a dram of..."

"Whoa, whoa, whoa," Angelo says, hooking a thumb at the Zonkey. "What the fuck is this guy talking about?" he asks

Chris, who shrugs. Angelo is ready, this time, and grabs the poofy thing to keep from falling over.

"My good man," the Zonkey says, nonplussed, "I am simply attempting to assist you in the..."

"Yeah, yeah," Angelo says. "Who did you say you were, again?"

"Why I am a Zonkey. The singularly unique offspring of a zebra and a donkey."

Angelo nods, "Right. Well, let me give you a little advice, pal..."

"Here it comes," Christopher Columbus tips a wink at Charlie and the regulars.

"...no one likes a smart ass," Angelo finishes.

"Zing!" says Charlie. Morrie smiles and goes back to his beer.

The Zonkey shakes his head. "This whole idiotic short story, all for that abominable punch line? Goodness, me!"

Chris gives Angelo a high-five, "I saw that one coming a mile away."

Angelo laughs. "Yeah. I was waiting for Charlie to hit him with, 'Hey, why the long face', you know?"

"Oh yeah," Charlie says, "That one's a classic. I wanted to see where you'd go with it, though. Good one, Ange. Now, what can I get you?" he says to the Zonkey.

"Ah well, a Manhattan for me then," the Zonkey sighs.

"Yeah," Angelo says, "I'll try one of them things."

"Coming right up," Charlie says, clinking ice cubes into a couple of glasses. "This one's on the house."

Sometime much later, Ring-A-Ding Lawrence yells "Ha! Funny joke!"

'Rot With Me'

by Anthony Rapino

They'd been here before. The stink of stale cigarette smoke and vomit. The quiet rage of accusation. The oppressive confinement of the car he drove. It was all too familiar, and it made John's head spin. He tapped the steering wheel and glanced over at Piper who noticed his expression not at all. He huffed and turned the heat up, then pulled off his wool hat and closed the passenger window, which even in the dead of winter Piper insisted on leaving wide open. Piper *ran hot*, she'd explained more than once, and usually John acquiesced. *Usually* he gave in.

Piper muttered something and her head lolled on her shoulders. Maybe she was asleep, but more likely she was trying not to allow conversation to surface. Her eyes fluttered open, though the lids remained droopy. She stared at John, her head still lopsided, her body hunched and crooked.

"You feeling okay, Pipe?"

She groaned and shifted to rest her head on the passenger door. A few of the wriggling worms that grew from her head screeched like cats, chilling John's already cold blood. Piper wouldn't have heard the screeches nor noticed the worms. That fresh hell was John's alone.

He bit down on air. He had this sudden urge to lean over her hulking mass and swing open the door. She'd probably tumble out, never even attempting to save herself. And that's why he was still there, wasn't it? To save her? *Fuck it*, he thought. *I'm done saving the dead.* And maybe he really was this time, or maybe it was just another hateful gripe concerning the never ending bleakness of his relationship with Piper.

John slowed as he approached Piper's driveway. He pulled in, then hesitated with his hand over the gear shift. Piper hadn't noticed the car stopped. He waited one more beat, then put the car in park and killed the engine.

John touched her shoulder. "We're here."

She roused and sat up, put one hand on the door handle. The worms poked in and out of her head, coming up for air then ducking back into the relative safety of her cavernous skull. *They're not really there*, he reminded himself, though it did not stop their eternal dance.

"Should I come up?" John asked.

"You always do." She opened the door, but didn't get out.

"Forget it."

"It's fine. It's just—"

"I know. I don't care."

They both exited and headed to the apartment building. Really, it was just a house that had been broken up into three apartments by floor. Piper's was on the third. The climb up the stairs was excruciating. Whether she really couldn't summon the energy or she was drawing it out purposely, John did not know.

Each stair she conquered caused a shockwave of relentless loathing to ripple through his veins. Darkness had crept into his life and eroded everything good. He used to start his mornings with a cup of coffee on his deck and stare out into the woods behind his house. This act of communion colored each day with earthy greens and browns. John's hours were those of endless wonder. He couldn't remember the last time he'd indulged in his morning routine.

At the door to her place, she turned. "It's bad."

"I know. You said."

She unlocked the door and they entered.

John stopped only a few steps in as an invisible wall fell atop him. The place reeked of rum and vomit. Yes, she had warned him, but *Jesus*. He'd been in dive bars that smelled better. He'd been in dive bar *bathrooms* that smelled better.

Piper escaped to her bedroom. As John walked further into the apartment, he reeled against its utter degradation. Vomit caked Piper's couch, which she had just purchased a couple weeks earlier. Empty bottles of rum littered the living room, as did dirty plates, empty bags of chips, DVD cases, and all manner of clothing.

As John inspected the debris, he hoped to God he wouldn't spot condom wrappers, but he didn't count it out. It'd be just like Piper to leave something like that around and then invite her boyfriend up for a visit. Then he stopped himself and chided. This wasn't a visit. And who knows if he was still her boyfriend. After what had happened last night, after the past month of this fucked up bullshit excuse for love. Yeah. It was anyone's guess.

Piper came back from her bedroom shaking her head. "Do not go in there."

Jealousy surfaced again. "Why? What is it?

Piper pushed back her greasy blonde hair. The worms luxuriated in her brief touch. "I puked in my sleep the other night. Fucking lucky I didn't drown in it. It's all over the bed and wall. Plus the blood and stuff. Just don't go in there."

"Damn, I'm sorry. I don't know--"

She laughed. It was unpleasant. "Don't fucking apologize. I put you in that situation. I've put *a lot* of people in that situation. It's what I do."

"I didn't have to call the cops though."

"You thought I was dead. I made you think I was dead." She laughed again.

John's insides felt as cold as her apartment. "How much was the hospital fee?"

"More than I can afford." The worms extended from her head at that taste of passive aggression. They loved it. Lapped it up the way Piper lapped up rum. A few got overexcited and spilled from their tiny holes, falling to the floor with little wet slaps.

"How long have you been off the wagon?"

She kicked an empty bottle as she walked to the kitchen. She opened the fridge door.

John didn't move from his station in the living room. In her tiny shit-shack, he didn't have to.

Head still in the fridge, she said, "I don't know. A week. Two. The fuck you care anyway?" She reentered with a bottle of beer and drank half of it in one shot. She stared at John, daring him to say something. "If you cared, you'd have been

76

here."

"You said you wanted space."

Her laugh split him in two. "You don't know shit about addicts. If you were here. If you lived here. That'd be the only way." She drank more. Spit on her floor. Kicked garbage around. "But you're too big a pussy."

This easy slide from one personality to another was one John had become all too familiar with. His face burned. He bit down on nothing and tried holding it all in. Piper had tried to kill herself, and it hadn't been the first time. He couldn't be blunt. He couldn't get angry. Who knew what would set her off again? With this spinning around his fire pit of a brain, he tried to pull it all back down. He jumped on top of the heap of grievances and attempted to compact it into the insubstantial receptacle, but his feet slipped, and he fell.

"Fuck you, Piper! Seriously, just—*fuck off.*"

She pulled the bottle away from her mouth. Bugs spilled over her lips, hitting the floor like a cascading waterfall. They skittered over her feet, up her legs. Piper didn't seem to notice.

"Shit," John said and backed away.

"Why don't *I* fuck off? This is my place! Why don't *you* fuck off!?"

The worms danced.

"Piper—" What was he going to say? He didn't want to be there. He *wanted* to leave. There was precious little keeping him there. Even his desire to save this broken girl had begun to fade after months of brick wall after brick wall.

Her arms split where the bandages were wrapped. Scars tore open to reveal muscle and vein. Piper said, "What?"

John bumped into the front door. Apparently he'd been backing away the whole time. He put his hand on the doorknob. "I love you, but I fucking *hate* you."

He turned away before she could respond and retreated through a door he hoped never to see again. The stairs were a blur. The world had lost its definition.

He opened his car door and barely noted the stale smell of vomit as he got in.

Piper stood in the same spot he'd left her moments before.

John's hand was extended with his car key, ready to start a car that he was not in. He felt dizzy. There were a lot of thoughts going through his head, but he was able to voice none of them.

"Well?" Piper now had a glass of rum. She drank, then sat on the soiled sofa. Blood leaked from her nose.

John was about to tell her as much when he realized it wasn't blood at all, but black leeches, and they just kept coming. "*This* is new."

She squinted at him, apparently not sure to what he was referring. In absence of understanding, she gave him the finger.

It was becoming too much for John. Not getting flipped off; he was used to that. But losing moments of time, appearing back in the apartment after getting into his car, the leeches pouring from Piper's nose? Bad signs, all of them. Sure, he'd questioned his sanity plenty of times before, what with the whole worm-head situation, but somehow he'd managed to keep it all hidden under the surface. Because even then, the worms weren't his first hallucination.

In his last relationship, he'd witnessed a multitude of squirming, furry creatures crawl into Vanessa's pussy. Like fanged teddy bears with oozing cocks, they clawed her open and dug inside, burrowing in completely, never to return. She of course didn't notice a thing. John had not been able to touch her after the bizarre occurrence, but it didn't matter, because she broke up with him soon after. Apparently she'd been cheating on him for months, and enjoyed the shit out of confessing moments before she left forever.

Before Vanessa there was Mindy, who'd let hundreds of tiny, voracious insect-like inhabitants chip away at her teeth. A month later she left John for a fellow meth addict.

And no, John was not stupid. He'd made the connections between his hallucinations and the women he dated. Like some kind of madhouse version of divine intervention, he could see the Dear John letters before they came. Which is precisely why this time, he meant to take action. This time, he planned on doing the leaving.

So why had he been transported back into the stone-cold apartment with his stone-cold girlfriend? Why had the hallucinations only gotten worse?

In answer, Piper burped. Then laughed. Then drank the rest of her drink. Then burped again.

Not much of an answer.

The leeches had ceased their intrepid voyage and resigned themselves to latching onto her face and neck to commence feeding. They grew fatter with blood every minute.

John reached forward to brush away a few of the offenders who'd made way for Piper's split and bleeding forearms. When his fingers touched her, the skin melted away like candle wax, revealing musculature and pus.

He screamed.

Piper twitched away and dropped her empty glass to the floor. She stood from the couch and stared at him for a moment before plodding off to the kitchen, presumably for another drink.

With all that had occurred, John had to focus on only one goal, because to absorb everything would most likely result in a complete shutdown. So John chose his one focus: flight. He turned and escaped that dank hole before another twisted visage could manifest. He busted through the door and took the stairs two at a time. Outside, the cold air felt good on his face and he sprinted towards the car. He hoped for snow, that it might cover the dirty ground with its pure white and hide, at least for a little while, everything underneath. Just window dressing, but a much need respite from the everyday horrors.

When John came to his Honda--also once white, now coated with road-dirt and mud--he paused. It was important he was completely conscious of his actions from this point forth. He needed to mark every step taken. The last time he must have blacked out and walked back into the apartment, and there was no way he would do that again. So he stood a moment longer and took a breath. He let his heart slow. He noted the light breeze and the lone bird singing in the tree branches above his car.

He nodded. "Okay. I'm good. This is good." Slowly, he opened the car door. He peered inside. Everything looked normal enough. He took one more deep breath and entered the car.

"Well? You want the drink or not?" Piper held a glass filled with rum and coke out to John.

"Fuck!" He backed until he hit the door. "What the fuck!?" He turned and ran off again, running down the staircase for a third time, even though he'd only climbed it once. He sprinted headlong at the car and meant to dive in and race off as fast as possible, the opposite tactic from last time. He got as far as putting the key in the ignition when—

"Well then fuck you too!" Piper drank from his glass, then her own.

"No, no, no, no, no!"

He turned and fled. Door. Stairs. Car.

"No what?"

Door. Stairs. Car.

"Fine, don't talk to me."

John bent and leaned on his knees, trying to catch his breath. He coughed and some spittle flew from his mouth. When he straightened, he saw the leeches, fat with blood, still sucking away. He closed his eyes and asked, "Was I here this whole time?"

"What do'ou mean?" Piper's eyes were glassy and heavy-lidded.

"Did I leave the apartment at all since we got here?"

She waved a hand in a dismissive way, forgetting she held a

drink in both. Rum splashed over the rim. "Shut up. You never want to have fun, you stupid." She brought a cup to her mouth and one of the leeches detached and fell in. She drank it up in a large gulp.

John retched and watched pus leak from one skinless arm. "I'm sick. I don't know…ah, god. What the hell? What the fucking hell?"

Piper ignored this.

John fell to his knees and began crying. His face burned and the tears on his cheeks stung.

"Fuckin' pussy little pussy." Piper laughed. "Pussy!"

John was used to this. From passive aggressive to aggressive. The duality of Piper. It was like living with two different people. Hell, a *dozen* different people. She was drunk now, and she wanted a fight. She wanted John to yell and scream and call her names. And if he did, she'd lap it up like she did her booze until finally turning it all inward. She'd rip her own hair out and cry and punch herself and progress to cutting. Always cutting. It didn't matter if he rode out the spiteful curses and tried to soothe her, or if he gave in to anger and yelled. It didn't matter if he was there or not. She'd cycle through the same old routine one way or the other. Over and over and over. Frightful infinite insanity.

Piper screamed, "You hear me, pussy?" Worms fell from her hole-filled head. Leeches burst on her face, leaving huge red birthmarks behind. Pus built up under the skin and poured from her as she rotted before his eyes.

"Just stop, Piper. Please, will you stop?" He didn't know exactly what he meant. Stop drinking, yes. Stop yelling, certainly. Stop being a fucking lunatic, most definitely. Just stop everything.

And maybe Piper wasn't so drunk after all, because her response was pointed, as if she'd inferred it all. She leaned forward and held his gaze. She said, "*Never.*"

John stood and wiped away tears. "I want to leave, you understand? I *want* to go. But I can't. It won't let me." He didn't know why he was telling her this. She wouldn't understand. He needed medical attention. A therapist or a hospital or *something*.

Surprising him one last time, Piper said, "I know."

He stared at her, mouth hanging open, unsure of what to say.

Piper reached up and deliberately plucked a worm from her skull. She held it out between pointer and thumb, then dropped it in her mouth. She chewed, swallowed, then drank some more.

She had interacted with his hallucination. How? Was this all a hallucination? A dream? What? He said, "Did you—?"

"Yes."

"Yes what?"

"Unbelievable. You're not seeing things." She picked off a leech and flicked it at John.

His head felt like a top. He didn't know what to believe anymore, and it didn't bother him at all because there was only one thing he wanted. "Let me go then. I want to *go*."

Piper got close and he could smell dead meat. "You already

made your choice, and it was to stay. It's too late to go back now."

"No." He pushed her, trying to keep the stench away. "I told you I wanted to leave, I *did* leave."

"This time, sure." She chuckled and blood gurgled up through her mouth. "You work up the balls to leave about once every thousand times."

"What is this—?"

"*Think*, stupid. I'm getting tired of explaining it."

John did that. He thought. He thought hard. "Hell?"

Piper laughed, bringing up more blood. She gagged, then vomited red. When she was done, she snagged a bottle from the floor and drank long. "No, we're not in *Hell*. We're in a *relationship*. And you picked the *wrong—fucking—girl*."

She dropped the bottle and pushed John against the wall. Blood and pus and insects all soaked his clothes. She pushed her whole mushy, stinking body against his, and god help him, he got hard. She licked his face. "You're mine, sissy boy. You've always been mine. When I'm Vanessa. When I'm Mindy. You're *mine*."

Piper reached down the front of his pants and grabbed his hard cock. Her loose, rotting skin peeled as she gripped him. He wasn't trying to get away any more. He was grinding up against this corpse. The dirt and vomit coated his face. He let it fall into his mouth as she jerked him off.

She spit on him, and he said, "Fucking cunt!"

"That's right. Who am I?"

"You're a cunt! My fucking cunt girlfriend."

"You see? You stupid shit. *Mine!*" She redouble her grip and yanked harder.

He buried her face into her leech-covered neck. He smelled rot and rum and blood, all of it somehow sexual. He groaned, "Oh shit."

Hearing this, Piper withdrew her hand, which no longer had skin attached.

John frowned. "I was about to cum."

Piper smiled a bloody gash. "I know."

John reached out to touch her, to draw her near again, when he became lightheaded and toppled forward—

The stink of stale cigarette smoke and vomit. The quiet rage of accusation. The oppressive confinement of the car he drove. It was all too familiar, and it made John's head spin. He tapped the steering wheel and glanced over at Piper who noticed his expression not at all.

They'd been here before.

Piper's head lolled on her shoulders. She said, "Don't be sad, love. We'll always have each other."

'Edibility'

by Mercedes Yardley

"Tink electrocuted himself today. No joke. Remember the bobcat thrown over the power lines? Just like that. Tink climbed up there to see if things looked any different."

She was sitting in the flowers, eating petals. She examined each one individually before gently placing it on her tongue, closing her mouth and savoring.

"So the funeral is Thursday. The bobcat, right? Remember how it fell to the ground and started on fire? Man, I never thought I'd see anything like that again! And now Tink. It was just awesome."

They had a lawn once, but she had pulled it all out, first by hand and then with a shovel. She had lain in the black dirt, sucking at the grass roots in search of nectar she never found. Then she had pulled seeds out of her pockets, all manner of seeds. No grass now, only flowers.

"The guys are going out to shoot pool tonight, wanted to know if I'd come. I said you wouldn't mind. You don't mind, do you, baby? I thought not. I'll bring something home when I come. Something with pecans for the morning. I'll make it good."

She was baking lemon cakes today, but he didn't notice or didn't care, and this did not bother her. She stood up, carefully picking her way through the flowers, a bunch of purple and yellow johnny-jump-ups in her hand. He tromped over the flowers, crushing blooms as he went, but it was all right. She could get them to raise their heads again.

"So, later, darlin'. Don't stay up too late. I'll get back when I get back."

He pressed a kiss into her hair, and she smiled at him. The flowers screamed as he headed to the car, but she gave them a little wink, and they calmed.

The lemon cakes were shaped like stars. They cooled on the windowsill because this house was their own little suburbia, and such things were allowed. She removed the heads of the johnnys and floated them in a bowl of chilled water.

She mixed together powdered sugar and milk, added vanilla and frosted the cakes. She carefully laid the johnnys side by side on a clean dish towel to dry.

The cat wrapped around her leg. She sent it outside to chase the flowers, who squealed merrily when the cat batted at their petals. The cat hummed.

Once dry, she sprinkled the johnnys on the star cakes. The cakes were beautiful, cheery little things, and she waited for somebody to come by and ask for one. Somebody always did.

Two goldfish swam in a bowl resting in the hollowed out TV. "Shhh," she whispered to the bigger one, who was complaining. She crumpled up a little bit of cake in her hands, let it fall into the water like sand. The johnny-jump-ups swirled across the top of the water to their own music.

She curled up in the chair, slipped a blanket over her translucent body. She opened a book but didn't read, instead running her hand across the words on the paper. If she took scissors, cut the paper into the shape of a mask and peered through, what would she see? What would she see?

'Cut the Cord'

by Val Tenterhosen

People are always like "Scram, scram, scram!" I leave my door open in hope and they're like "Shut it!" I don't have to butter my bread twice to know *they're* the lonely ones. But hearing their screams really makes me blue, inside.

I did something about it once. Something deep. Something really rolled up tight, like a newspaper when it comes time to thwack the doggie. I knew what I had to do, but once I was finally finished, it didn't seem so cut and dried. I started to worry.

I started drinking. Things just didn't have no fun in it no more. I tried barley, I tried rye. I tried a shot at all the things they told me would make it better. It didn't make it better. I felt lower and lower. It began to spiral.

I needed out. So I did the only thing I had left to do: I did it again. And again. And again. And it didn't make it better, it just made it harder. Harder not to do it: again and again and again. So I tried to make it be easy again.

I tried doing it more. And that didn't help neither. All it did was make it easier than not doing it. It became a way of life. It became a way *out* of life. It became all I had left. Which is funny, in a way. Because when I started out doing it, I thought the same thing.

It all comes 'round in the end. And it always does, whatever you might think. One day, it came around to me. And then that's all there was, you might say.

Because beside this silly little note, that *is* all there was. They found me. They're busting in right now. And they want to do to me what I did to all those folks that got in my way. That I *put* in my way. All because of one little jar I forgot to wash out.

They can get you with almost anything these days. It's a kind of curse. It's kind of a curse. It's the kind of thing they do to a fellow when they know what he's done.

They judge him, son. They judge him.

'One Evening with the Midnight Company'

by M.C. O'Neill

It's spring!

Clammy evening air foretold of the coming thunderstorm and anyone in our business knew that such weather was perfect for taking one of those awful beasts down. These foul things thrived in the springtime as this was their holy season or some such nonsense. Jumping and playing in the ragweed and pollen. Beautiful harbingers of hayfever. The rain would only draw them out as they loved to dance in it like raving lunatics. Even at night.

Hells, she probably wouldn't even see us as she would be sure to be indulging in her happy fugue. Twirling, spinning and laughing as she soaked in the nature. *Creep*. Tonight, we would have the initiative. Tonight, we would slay a dryad.

* * *

Buckles O'Botis, my stoutkin assistant, lounged back in the bucket seat of the hatchback. He closed his eyes for a second and let loose a big one. Fat little bastard.

"By the gods, Buckles!" I winced as the aroma from his backside wafted over to my nose. "What in the hells did you eat? *Damn* you!"

Giggling like an idiot, the wee one had signed my name on that odorous sweet nothing. He always knew how to disgust me, and if he wasn't attempting to make me sick with his gastrointestinal acrobatics, he was certain to try to get my goat.

"Oh, just keeping you on your toes, Cal!"

I growled through gritted teeth while rolling down the window. His bowels were murderous. "Do you think you could wait until we got out of the car? Good gods, at least save it for the job!"

By the way, Buckles was one-half of The Amity Midnight Company LLC. Calvin Amity, that being my name and my father's before me. Why I had taken that curly-headed geek on as my sidekick is too long of a story to tell, but despite him always antagonizing me, as stoutkin are wont to do, I must say I owed him one. Truth be told, I owed him quite a few as I would have never survived any of our jobs on the lonesome. Yeah, I was sure of that.

Still wincing from the shock of the stench, I almost swerved the hatchback off the road as we rounded the wooded bend. My ratty mobile just didn't have the handling it used to. I delighted in seeing Buckles' eyes widen in momentary horror. Served him right.

"Yeah, but if I rip one on the job, she might hear us," he countered as he regained composure.

Still revolted, I squeezed my nostrils. My voice sounded like I had devoured a quart of helium for supper. "Well, she sure-as-hells would *smell* you, you rotten little worm!"

Ignoring my banter, Buckles hopped in his seat and pointed out the passenger window like his ass was on fire, which it probably was. "Cal!" he squealed. "Hard right!"

Years of sharpened reflexes (more like nerves), prompted me

to act before questioning the little guy and my body obeyed his warning before my mind could protest. Always the perceptive one, he caught the turnoff in the dwindling gloom of the early evening.

Lights from the tavern flooded our car's cabin at the very instant I had completed my dizzying turn. It was no wonder I hadn't caught it, as the place was nestled in a grove of towering oaks which shielded the glow from the main road. Ground to a halt, I could see that I had almost careened my car into a posh, silver coupe. It wouldn't surprise me if its owner was an elf.

"Whoa!" Buckles moaned in his usual high pitch. For a second, he sounded to me like a confused child. "That was a close one! If you had hit that roadster, we'd be in the hole! Everyone knows an elf would sue your ass off faster than rabbits make love in the spring. And another thing…"

"You think I don't know that?" I cut him off, angry. "Maybe if you'd paid more attention to navigation than giving me the ol' gas attack, you could have caught the turnoff in better time! They don't call this dump 'Secret Paradise' for nothing!"

"Yeah, but…"

"Look," I adjusted myself behind the steering wheel. "Let's just find a parking spot and figure out a solid plan for tonight. I'm not getting rabies again like I did on the last job! I was stuck in that goofy monastery for nearly four weeks recuperating. Not fun, buddy. All that chanting day and night gave me the willies."

His humor disarmed, the stoutkin threw out his hands in defeat. "Fine, boss. Suit yourself."

The lot of Secret Paradise was packed. It took almost five

minutes to find a vacant spot for our subcompact. Milling hither and yon was the local nightlife of the surrounding area. Many of them were mercenaries and other wayfarers who were ambling about in their stupors. They probably had just returned from jobs of their own and were making the time to celebrate their upcoming windfalls. For the moment, I was a bit jealous of them. Clutches of honeyed elves strode into the tavern like they owned the place, or anywhere else for that matter. Gods, I could never stand elves.

"Okay," I grunted as the car's motor died. "Let's do the big check."

Popping the hatchback, we made inventory of all the necessities. Although Buckles could be the bearer of foul shenanigans, I had to give it to him that he was mighty organized. The boot of the car looked like a surgical display of battle. A veritable mobile quartermaster's.

First aid kits, glowsticks, canvas gloves, two walkie-talkies, a machete, lanterns, various ropes and bungee, webbing, and, of course, a pair of gorgeous ballbats were installed onto the upholstery like a tight showroom panorama. Sloshing in a five-gallon plastic tank off to the side was tonight's secret weapon: Condensed Agent Orange. Two gas masks dangled from the back door.

"Hey, Buckles," I huffed. "Where's the hose and nozzle for the Orange? Don't expect me to sneak up behind that creep and just dump it on her head. This stuff will make you glow in the dark!"

"Eh, that's under the webbing. Coiled it myself last night."

Double-checking his report, I saw the glint of the nozzle blinking in the pink light of the tavern's marquee. "Cool. Good enough for me. I think we're all set, mate."

"Great!" Buckles beamed. "Let's get in there and find a boo͜t͜h before they're all taken. I'm starving! I really don't want to discuss business up at the bar. You know, prying ears and whatnot."

I slammed the trunk shut and gave the latch a second tug to make sure all was secure; I gave the old mobile a slap on its posterior for luck. "All right, little man. Let's get some slaying fuel in us."

* * *

Look, there's one thing you need to know about stoutkin. I don't mean to be all stereotypical or anything like that, but this pretty much describes the little buggers across the board: they call it as they see it.

Never had I met one to have any bout of fear that lasted for more than a minute. It's almost as if they forget they're in danger even while in the clutches of some terrible monster. As such, they aren't the most diplomatic of folk, and sometimes, Buckles would take advantage of that ingrained trait and would aggravate me just for the sake of doing so.

Oh, and another thing—they're all from Ireland. Don't ask me why, but I've never met a stoutkin that didn't hail the Emerald Isle as his home.

He had predicted right, though. The place was bustling and the jukebox was spinning that droning techno crap that I just *knew* an elf had put into the queue. I'm old school. I need some rock and roll or even a good, solid country tune when I've had a few pints. This fancy dreck buzzing through the air was only working my nerves all the more.

..e tavern, a booth full of snooty elves
.pensive) gear and preparing to leave
.vas for one of their dowdy parties in one
.ns down by the lake where they'd drink
.e wine all night.

..ed up to them in grand style as they lifted their
lithe bo.. ..d gave them an impatient huff. Not one of them
seemed amused by this. Good job, Buckles.

"Ewl, look!" one of their lot's females oozed. She was
dressed in a gossamer maxi-dress that left little to the
imagination in its sheer. "It's a wee one from Eire!"

Her accompanying throng of four chortled at her moronic
humor. Two of her laddie-friends clinked together their empty
wine (of course) glasses.

"And now, what would ye be doin' in these parts o' the
woods, ye wee, fat fecker?" she mocked my mate in a phony
stoutkin accent as she stooped to his height. To be expected, her
plush peanut gallery cheered her antics on.

Buckles wasn't my assistant's real name, in case you're
wondering. Few stoutkin ever use their birth names as almost
all of them earn goofy monikers in their youths for some reason
or another. Buckles had gotten his on account of all the hidden
blades he'd been known to strap about his person since he was
but a teen on the streets of Donegal. Life for a young thief could
be tough there, so I've been told time and again.

Within the flash of a sudden blackout, one of these said
blades was pressed against the long throat of the racist reveler.
Stoutkin may forget to be afraid, but anger can smolder inside
of them for a bit longer and the look on my partner's normally-
cherubic mug had grown murderous.

"You take that back and we'll take your seats! Got it, wench?"

Elves just aren't used to such roughhousing, I laughed to myself as I soaked in the fear on their faces. The lady looked like she was about to have an asthma attack as Buckles held her in place with a tug of her voluminous, red hair. Her tender laddie-friends gasped in unison and knew not what to do but stare on in terror. Not one of this crew had seen a single minute of real adventure in their lazy lives, and this was obvious.

"Ew! Ew!" she bleated. "I — I take it back! I take it all back!" She pronounced "all" as "aul." Ridiculous.

As his rage subsided, the stoutkin retracted the dagger and shoved the elfmaid out of the booth's space. Her buddies couldn't wait to follow her lead and appeared quite comical as they rushed past us in their horror. At times like this, I envied Buckles' bravery, which, I must admit, I've never had a large supply of.

"Right, then," he puffed as he situated himself in the booth. He was the boss for that moment and I couldn't bear to doubt his authority. Not that elves were anything to get worked up over. I'm sure I could have licked them even at my age.

"Good riddance to bad trash, eh?" I agreed with him as I joined him on his opposite end. "I'd say you handled that pretty well, mate. Nice and clean."

"Aye," he confirmed. His breathing was still a bit labored from the recent action. "But I do wish a busser would come around and do away with this foofy nonsense left on our table."

In a gesture of gratitude, I shoved the elves' leavings aside to clear out our space. At that moment, the mindless repetition of the techno tune segued into the strains of fiddling of a proper stoutkin folk song. I didn't really know which was worse, as the songs of Buckles' countryfolk had always reminded me of a line of riverdancers. Sometimes, I would envision these dancers exploding due to spontaneous combustion one-by-one as they pranced in place without care. Regardless, Buckles seemed to be cheered by this turn of audial event and that was fine by me.

As our ales replaced the empty wine glasses and brandy snifters, I gave Buckles a look of solid business. It was time to sort out the operation for tonight before the drink took one or the both of us over and we would be apt to forget the entire thing in our drunken fugs. This meant not getting paid.

"Look," I leaned in. "This job should take nothing more than flashlights, masks, slickers and the Orange. Real quick and easy, like. We drive to the Appledoor Grotto, get in, blast her, and then get the hell out of there before we ourselves dissolve into slag."

My mate's wispy brows furrowed in contention. "See, that's what's been bothering me about this shindig. You've brought up a good point."

"Bother you?" I banged the table. "She's just a dryad! We can fog the whole place to Kingdom Come! She'll never know what hit her."

Buckles rolled his eyes. It was apparent I didn't get his gist.

"But that's my point!" he protested. "Appledoor Grotto is a Dutch national landmark! Now, I know you Americans care nothing for the environment, but the government of South Holland does! We spray this crap all over the place—we'll not only kill the dryad, but we'll wilt the entire site!"

Over in the back of the bar, a rowdy lot of mercenaries were playing a ridiculous drinking game. I had no clue what the rules of it were, but the woman in their group was crushing a lemon within her flexed bicep. Its juice was running down into her unshorn armpit while one of her comrades had to lap up the sluice. Vile, I thought. After giving them a good glance, I recognized their bunch as a clutch of sell-guns from Germany. *Heinrich's Hailstorm*, I believe was their name. According to the industry scuttlebutt, they specialized in icing vampires. Crazy fools.

"So, what does McCullough think about it?" I countered. "He doesn't care about a few wasted chipmunks and some dead apple trees. All that matters to him is a dead dryad and we are going to hand our boss a dead dryad, you dig?"

"McCullough is slime," Buckles clucked. "That bastard would strap his own mother to a nuke for five Krugerrands. When the Dutch authorities, or even *Interpol* come banging on our flat, he certainly won't back us up!"

Doctor Davis McCullough *was* a slime, Buckles was correct about this, but the old geezer got us the jobs. He got us the good jobs that you still had a prayer of walking away from with your head intact. Sure, I didn't like that lout personally, but he kept my bills paid. Buckles was just looking a gift horse in the mouth. Those stoutkin were fearless, yes, but they were also a bit too considerate for their own good—especially when it involved nature.

"Buckles," I said, attempting to regain my authority. "Nobody likes their boss. But you have to suck it up and roll with the punches. McCullough gets us the sweet assignments and pays on time. He's never screwed us over with remittance."

The stoutkin began to chuckle in triumph like he had just

beaten me at a hand of poker. "McCullough gets us the *easy* jobs because he knows you're a chicken. I mean, come on! Dryads? My grandmother could lick one of those things and go back to darning socks."

That remark had hit me like a two-by-four to the face. I hated it when Buckles was right about such stuff. I am a chicken, it's true. When I looked over again to Heinrich's Hailstorm's revelry, I couldn't help but note their top-of-the-line gear and boisterous sense of well-being. Those guys were happy. They were secure in their abilities, and thus, reaped the spoils of their joy. Assholes.

When Buckles got on a roll, you just had to let him keep on going until he was finished. That stoutkin possessed the gift of gab and onward he *would* gab. Even when he chewed you out, his lilt sounded kind of nice to my American ears. Hurtful, but nice.

"And you know this!" Buckles laughed at me in spite. "McCullough doles out these pee-wee jobs to us because he knows what a tired, old dog you are. You've been scared shitless of shadows your entire life and you float your damn organs like a jakey all the time just so you can cope with the adventure! You're a joke of a wayfarer and I know the boss laughs at us for it! We could be like Heinrich's Hailstorm back there, delving into disused mansions and staking vampires for the big bucks, but you'd rather take these penny-ante tasks that an old lady could finish before settling down to a romance novel. Calvin Amity… 'Calamity'?' My arse!"

That did it. That little twerp was giving me too much lip for his own good.

In the wayfarer business, I had garnered the nickname "Calamity" over the years. It was a portmanteau of my given name and my surname, but held the connotation of humiliating irony due to my "soft" assignments. Everyone in the industry knew what a milquetoast I was and my contemporaries had made a good laugh of it. It was so sad to hear my partner of eleven years feed that fire.

"Low blow, Buckles," I defended as I pulled another drink. "Dryads are as just as dangerous as a damn vampire. We could wind up with half the grotto's animals attacking us from her freaking pheromone control. Those critters love her! I mean, how would you like to have a torrent of squirrels and shit drowning us in rabid bites? Maybe even a wolf or two?"

"Dryads," he puffed. "Ratkin, nymphs, sylphs, and now — dryads. Do you get the picture? Look at all these ponce jobs we get! And all the beasts we slay are usually female to boot! I'm not surprised we don't have feminist organizations protesting us."

"Hey, now. That nymph had to go!" I resolved. "She would prance around the streets of Toulouse all day buck naked, blinding any fool who dared to look at her! *'Ew! Look at my boobs! Look at my boobs!'* Sure she had great breasts, but that's all part of a nymph's game. We had to take her out. Half the men of that burg are still in recovery! And don't get me started on those ratkin."

"Oh, you mean poor Candrella," Buckles attempted to shame me. "She was only doing what she does naturally and we had to snuff her out simply for some credit. Just because a lady likes to run about in the buff doesn't mean she deserves a death warrant."

"It does when she cripples the male populace of a mid-sized city while doing it!" I was fuming. Buckles had assisted in that job with as much gusto as had I.

Candrella LeViere was a nymph who had just reached sexual maturity about two years ago. For the bulk of her life, she had lived in a forest right outside of Toulouse, France, but once she had hit puberty, she wanted to show the world her goods.

Although quite the spectacle, a nymph's wanton nudity could pose a problem for the male gentry. These beasts are so beautiful that the heterosexual human male would lose his eyesight upon witnessing such an exhibit. Lucky for me, Buckles wasn't human.

It was an easy operation. Too easy. That stunning demon was jumping around the alleys and thoroughfares of Toulouse without a stitch, singing "Oh-la-la!" and all that tripe whilst any man in her eyeshot lost their sense of sight. Terrible.

Enter Buckles. I couldn't do any of the wetwork on that job because I too would have become blinded. Stoutkin are immune to nymph beauty and it took no time for the wee one to sneak in for the kill.

I hid up in a bell tower, just beyond her range of effect. Despite the distance, I still had the opportunity to enjoy an eyeful of that monster's grace and gorgeousness. Even from that length, I had fallen into her lovely spell.

Her rump was like a sweet pumpkin and her breasts defied all gravity. No matter how much she pranced and danced, that bosom would remain in firm place. She would swirl and twirl her bountiful blonde hair like molten gold as she frolicked. What a happy idiot she was and we had been commissioned to end her gaiety — permanently.

To be honest, I couldn't get the memory of that assignment out of my head. I would have used my Lee Enfield sniper's rifle for a fast, merciful kill, but spotting her through a scope would have blinded me as well. Buckles had to get in up-close and personal.

The little geek ran behind Candrella quick and disabled her flashing power by enveloping her in a canvas bag. By the time he began to beat her senseless with a ballbat, her wonderful songs of woo had ended. I wished that the sack hadn't been white. The nymph's blood was soaking it red within seconds as he busted her body asunder and I had felt so sick from the sight of it.

"And you pummeled the crap out of her, if I remember correctly. McCullough got his nymph and the city of Toulouse was safe once again. I rest my case."

The wee stoutkin bristled. He knew I had won at that moment. "It still was a chickenshit job and I took no joy in bashing that sweet maiden apart like I did. She just wanted to express herself."

"Sure!" I argued. "At the expense of…"

Heinrich von Lindsenmann and company were upon us. His troupe of wayfarers blotted out the lights of the tavern as they surrounded our booth. This was going to be a good one.

They were all bedecked in the finest of leathers and straps. Pinewood stakes and real silver daggers adorned their accoutrements. The woman who had lemon juice cascading down her exposed ribs was donning an haute Armani leather jerkin.

"So," Heinrich sang to me in his Teutonic clip. "Looks like Calamity is getting ready for some big business. What is on the menu for tonight? Maybe cockroaches, eh?"

At that, his cadre laughed like bumptious boors. Even if I

was amongst them, I would not have found his wit very funny. Ah, Germans…

'Oh, that was a real knee-slapper, Heinrich," I scowled. "Yeah, I'm on a job tonight, but I've left all the bloodsuckers for you. After all, it takes one to know one."

That was a good comeback. Heinrich's Hailstorm was not known for their ethics. Sure, they were prompt, as Germans are wont to be, but the word on the wire was that they were known to skim from the finances. Even McCullough was hip to their business practices and avoided assigning them work. More for me and Buckles, I supposed.

"Perhaps we are bloodsuckers," the German chuffed. "But at least we aren't bloody cowards. Look at your gear, mate. Where did you get it from? Tesco's?"

Another round of supportive laughter burst upon his cue. He had his clowns trained well.

"No, you fascist asshole, I got it at Sainsbury's."

Now his glee club was laughing *with* me at my counter. This did not amuse the big man and I could see his shadow looming over me ever the closer.

"It is lucky for you, Calamity, that we are in a public forum, *Ja?*" Heinrich's menace was much too near for my nerves. His breath stank of bratwurst and pilsner. "Otherwise, I would crush you and that stoutkin stooge of yours like the bugs you are paid peanuts to hunt."

Out of one eye, I had to capture Buckles' reaction to that remark. He looked like his head was ready to pop from the pressure of unabated rage. At that moment, I knew I had to get on the clock. My partner was not going to let this one slide. No one was allowed to insult his intelligence.

By the time I matched Heinrich's gaze once again, I noticed how his haughty bravado had frozen into shock. That look on his face was priceless as Buckles' blade was soon thrust against the lout's crotch. Gods, that stoutkin was fast.

"How'd you like to try to crush me without your bollocks, *Ja*?"

Unlike our scrap with those elves, Heinrich's goons were not deterred with such ease. Their group of five growled in unison at Buckles' threat.

Reveling in his angry daze, Buckles hissed at their lot. "Back away, all of you. You come any closer or touch Calvin, Heinrich will be pissing through a tube for the rest of his life."

Of course, this development would only prove to add to my legendary cowardice, as a mere stoutkin had to save my neck from the bullying of the Hailstorm Company, but I cherished my skin more so than my reputation. I could just imagine their crew chortling like high-school bullies as they drove away in equal parts triumph and shame. Yes, it would be a defeat for them, but a comedic one at my expense.

"Now," Buckles continued with his warning. "I want all of you morons to hop in your shiny little SUV and motor far away from here.

They sauntered off upon this impasse. Not one of them would tear their menacing gloat from me. These guys weren't elves and they would never be the kind of folk to run away from anything in terror.

One of their numbers, I never caught his name, thrust a finger at me as he swaggered on.

"Better you sleep with one eye open from now on, Chickenshit Amity. We're gonna get you."

He was a young buck and would have no problem scrapping with an old goat like me. I could only hope against hope that he never made it back from one of his future jobs. Like the rest of the Hailstorm, he was pipes-and-wires hard and I'd have no chance against him in a proper fight.

Tugging on my goatee, I tried to disguise my shivers, but Buckles could detect that my hackles were on high alert. I had always hated him seeing me like this, which was quite frequent.

"Don't worry about him, Calvin," he said, already cooled down. It was remarkable how he could rebound in such little time. "I think our little encounter won't remain on their minds for long. The Hailstorm are a busy crew."

"Yes," I agreed. "It's good to be rich and successful. I can only imagine."

Sinking his final swig of ale, Buckles slapped the rim of the stein for luck. Oh, the Irish.

"Right, then," I said. "Speaking of riches, however small they might be, I suppose we ourselves best be off. It's bad enough it'll be pitch dark out there, but we'll be soaked to the bone by the time we get there."

I turned my sights to the tavern's door, beyond which our adventure beckoned. Even with the drink in me, the pre-job jitters still jumped around in my guts. I shut my eyes for a second and prayed a mantra in silence: "*It's only a dryad, it's only a dryad.*"

* * *

My hands were shaking and I had to strangle the steering wheel or else I was apt to go spastic. Just something to hang onto. The drive-up was always the worst part of any job. Every time we'd motor to a site, I wanted to vomit or even fall asleep. It was like I could hope for some last-minute excuse to call the whole thing off. But, as they say, there're no sick days in the wayfarer business.

About the job. This dryad went by the name of Heike Nutcorn. All dryads were called upon by some type of arboreal moniker and Heike was no exception.

She reared her leafy head about a month ago in the Appledoor Grotto. Under normal circumstances, this was a government-protected tourist garden. People, usually wealthy people, from all over the world would flock to point at the flowers and go, "Ew... look!" Ever since Ms. Nutcorn had set up shop there, the place was in total chaos.

Dryads hated humanity, and this was no myth. Imagine the most extremist animal rights activist and multiply that anger by one hundred and you'll have a typical dryad. In some ways, considering how we humans routinely damage the environment, I couldn't blame the creeps in their spite for us.

I wasn't messing around when I had claimed that they could be just as vicious as a vampire. These creatures were known to shoot spores which could blind, poison or even disease a human being. Along with these clouds, they could also fire volleys of venomous thorns, the effects of which could paralyze the human nervous system.

One of their deadliest forms of defense was their ability to control the animals of the area to do their bidding via a strange pheromone manipulation. To imagine being stunned helpless while a coterie of woodland critters gnawed on your flesh is not a laughing matter when it's happening to you.

Already, five children had been bitten by her chipmunk slaves and an old dowager had been dive-bombed by a murder of remote-controlled crows. The birds had even gotten off with her pearl necklace, according to the latest reports. After that incident, the government had ordered the place closed down.

As we drove east through the winding wilderness roads, the thunderstorm was in full effect. The rain doused the windshield in pelting torrents and was peppered with small hailstones. It reminded me of some of the thunder-bumpers my family had suffered back home in the Kingdom of Indiana. Things were so much simpler for me back then.

When my pre-job anxiety was amped, I sometimes felt the impulse to shout, "Everything's gonna be okay!" at the top of my lungs. A nice tension breaker. At times like this, I would think about how horrible I am at my job and I just wanted to go to sleep.

"Calvin," Buckles warned. "We're almost a mile out according to the map. We'd better turn off the lights so we can sneak in."

He had a good point I had forgotten to consider as I pushed onward. A dryad could use her animal "friends" as lookouts and spies in order to gather intelligence of the local area. Few nightbirds were native to these parts of Holland, but there were always bats that could offer Heike some solid aerial recon. This could spoil our plans as we had wanted to rely on stealth.

"All right," I agreed. "It'll be a little rough going with all the rain, but I'll be careful. Take it slow."

My partner nodded. "I'll keep a lookout for any of the local nightlife. Raccoon, fox, deer, wolf. You know the lot. Last thing we need is some mind-controlled doe careening into the hatchback."

"Not fox," I blurted as I snapped off the headlights. "Not now."

"Why not?"

"Fox are crepuscular. They only romp around at dawn and dusk. It's too late now for fox."

Buckles settled back into the seat's bucket. "Well, then I suppose that's one less beastie we need to worry about. Oh! What about skunk?"

As if my nerves couldn't get any worse, he had to bring such things up. How awful it would be to have a platoon of those stinky creatures waiting for us ass-end first like an odorous firing squad.

"Yeah, they'll be up and running. I guess it's too late now to go back for noseplugs and lemon juice," I winced.

Although the sign was in Dutch, I could make out the lingo with ease. "*Appledoor Grotto: Volgende recht.*" Underneath the road marker, an alarming red notice hung, but I couldn't discern its message.

"Buckles, you know Dutch, yes?"

"A little," he answered. "Well, enough to get around."

"What's that sign underneath the road marker say?"

Craning his stumpy neck out the passenger window, the stoutkin squinted his eyes through the rushing rain. His curly, red hair was already soaked in that instant.

"It says, '*Currently condemned. Entry prohibited!*'" He had to shout over the bang of a tremendous thunderclap. The storm was only getting worse.

"That's kind of what I thought it said," I nodded, trying to hide my dread.

Without incident, we were soon upon our insertion point. Perhaps it was fate or just dumb luck, but we had managed to arrive to our destination unmolested by beast or bird. I killed the engine and let the hatchback coast into a silent, soft halt at the side of the road.

"Okay," I whispered. "Let's get in the gear and be quick about it. I don't think any of the dryad's spies are on to us. This is golden. We can get in through the apple orchard, hide out and look for that awful maiden, and then — *blammo!*"

"Good thing she can't control insects," Buckles shivered. "I'm not afraid of much, but those little buggers are so… alien, I suppose."

Once again, we popped the boot's door. The rain was drumming on our slickers' hoods and still their plastic couldn't forefend its chill. I prayed to the gods that the woodland beasts of the grotto were hiding out from the storm and would not catch sense of us. I've always liked the easy jobs.

Buckles went to grab the Orange, but his bare hands alarmed me. "Buckles!" I hissed. "Don't touch that crap without the gloves. That stuff's military grade!"

"Oh, too right." He shot me back a nervous smile. "Good call, boss."

"Put on the mask first," I hushed. "Just in case there's a leak in the container. I doubt it, but you never know."

As they always wrote in the mystery novels, everything was too quiet. It was only logical that the local wildlife were taking shelter from the storm, but not bug, not beast or bird could be heard. It was like the little bastards were waiting for us, and when the time was right, they'd pounce.

My assistant was strapping his webbing and making quite the racket doing it. We'd be certain to lose the initiative if his clamor was to alert Heike's furry little goons.

"Shh!" I buzzed through the gas mask. "Be careful! You'll blow our cover."

"What?" the stoutkin stopped, leaning in. "I can't hear you through your mask."

Great. One thing that could botch any job was a lack of communication, but Buckles did have a point. The GP-5 gas mask was a Holy Ukrainian Empire model that was cheap, easily available and rather effective for its low price. Always in the need to cut costs, this was the issue that I had bought. The only problem with the GP-5 was that it had no microphone and all conversations were downed to a muffle. The slashing of the rain had only compounded the problem.

I held an index finger to the knobby filter as I flashed Buckles the universal sign to keep mum. To pack it in, I shook my head.

Buckles nodded an affirmative and shot back a silent thumbs-up. Sliding his ballbat into his webbing with care, he continued to equip himself for the hunt. It was at this point that the drone of the storm was broken with a new noise from up in the tree line just beyond us.

"Hoo-hoo."

An owl. What better spy than an owl. Wonderful low-light vision. A head that can scan an area at almost three hundred sixty degrees and, of course, the benefit of an aerial view. To make matters worse, they could prove to be efficient attackers. At a full dive, one swipe from its talons could be the equivalent of six razor blades raking across your scalp at fifty miles an hour.

By instinct, we ducked together against the bumper of the car. We listened for over a minute in fear of another report from the bird, but only the din of the rain remained. That feathered fiend had flown off to snitch. Goodbye initiative.

I had never served in the military, but Buckles and I knew a few Army divisionary signals for communication when silence was golden or speech difficult. This situation was plagued by both factors.

Snapping my index finger toward the tree line in two quick successions, I indicated to my assistant to rush the grotto from the thick hedge and survey. I packed it in with a flat palm letting him know to keep low once the bush was breached.

He was small and nimble and such athletics were not above his abilities. Sure, watching his tiny, plump body scramble an inch from the ground was a bit comical, but he knew what he was doing and he was doing it well.

Within moments, he was ruffling back from the undergrowth. Being masked, I couldn't see his face, but I knew the look on it was grim.

Terrible. He flashed me five frantic open palms with both hands outstretched. We had a count of fifty waiting for us.

112

By instinct, I began priming the nozzle. The Orange was going to have to work or we'd be doomed, and this was certain. There was no way in the hells that we could take out Heike by surgical means now. That monster had summoned her unwelcoming committee and was prepared to give us the business.

The gods only knew what this party consisted of. It could have been wolves, deer, maybe even a bear. That blasted owl had informed on us at a moment's notice and we would need to engage in a manner that I had always dreaded: a stand-up fight.

We moved low. The slosh of the agent in its tank was below the crackle of the storm, but our webbing jingled against our buckles. Such commotion made no difference. Heike knew we were coming, but not with *what*.

Like idiots, and that we were, we took the front entrance to the grotto. Right beneath the gates (*Welkom bij Appledoor Grotto!*). Upon scanning the area, my guts dropped. I wanted to turn back and go home. Make it all right again and forget about everything.

Yes, there was a family of growling wolves. Yes, there were hissing raccoon and a cadre of puffed skunk, their tails reared in a line ready for biochemical assault, but the most jarring sight of it all was *her*.

Alien beauty spun and cackled at us upon our arrival. She *glowed*. My cheap, digital watch had just beeped the alarm announcing midnight. Heike Nutcorn pirouetted in angry challenge as she mocked us in her verdant glory. Leaves and thorns festooned her body and her hair was a tangle of wild, red vines. Her nudity was just barely masked by her body's natural foliage. Ending her dance with a graceful curtsey, she righted herself and flashed us a rude gesture with a thorny finger.

My hands were shaking like Heike's leaves as I aimed the nozzle at our enemies. A pneumatic whine assured me that the gear was prepped and ready to go. The pump's trigger felt so heavy, but I had to be strong for this. That clutch of wolves launched at once, serving as her zoological cavalry, and despite Buckles' politically-correct protests, I had to do the unthinkable or it would be our throats.

Gods bless the black market. Gods bless the Dow Chemical Company.

'Christmas with the In-Laws'

by Tom Bordonaro

McFadden pulled the arrow out of his leg and looked at the tip. If there was poison there, he couldn't tell. It was covered in blood, though. Of this he was certain. Upon closer inspection he thought he saw what might be brown sludge on the copper end of the arrow. McFadden couldn't remember what that part was called. The pointy bit.

He could remember hearing, however, that people in this part of the world sometimes dipped the pointy bit in their own feces. Better to infect the wound of whatever innocent creature they happened to be hunting. In this case, him. The fact that they would then usually eat the befouled object of the hunt, in McFadden's opinion, was disgusting. He didn't think they would be eating him but there was no real way to be sure.

He tossed aside the arrow and decided to check the wound itself. Pulling apart the hole in his trousers to check the hole in his leg proved futile; what with all of the red blood and red fur and bloody red fur he couldn't tell if there was shit in there or not. It hurt, though, and no doubt.

"It's *Christmas*, you twats!" he bellowed into the jungle. Since McFadden was British, he pronounced it with the 'a' as in 'ants'. Like the ones he was sitting in. Like the ones who were now storming furiously up his leg. Like the ones who were biting his naughty parts.

McFadden jumped up, slapping at his legs; a dervish in red fur and fake beard whirling about in the middle of a small green clearing. On any other occasion, bugs and humidity notwithstanding, it all would have been quite festive.

He pulled down his pants, quickly, and began swiping with both hands at the underside of his scrotum, sending ants flying. Anyone happening upon him at that point would have wondered how Father Christmas had fallen on such hard times and whether that had anything to do with the fact that he was apparently trying to juggle his own testicles.

Growing panicked, McFadden began to hop backwards until, unfortunately, his ankles caught a small, rotting log. A sudden crack and puff of splinters and the remaining ants were riding out of the clearing and down into the adjacent ravine at terrifying speeds on a bedraggled furry red luge which seemed to be powered at the front end by crass language. Everything his head hit on the way down knocked a "fuck!" out of McFadden and this was so often that it began to sound as if he was yelping one long curse word with thousands of syllables.

Somewhere ahead of him a small chameleon crawled lazily along a log looking for grubs. It turned its head slightly as the distant sound of something swearing and crashing through the jungle came rapidly down the hill. The sound got louder and suddenly McFadden and his ant passengers burst into sight and dopplered by...fuckfuckfuckfuck!...and disappeared again, heading down. The chameleon had followed all of this and now went stoically back to looking for lunch. Sometimes you just saw some odd shit in the jungle, was all.

Right after being spotted by the chameleon but before he came to a bouncing rest on top of the crocodile, McFadden lost his pants. The upside was that most of the ants were torn away with them. The downside was that he had no longer had any pants on.

At the bottom of the ravine was a river. In the river were

crocodiles. In one second one of them was sunning itself on the edge of the water and, in the next, there was something on its head. Something that was not a hat. Of course, the crocodile had no idea what a hat was. Still, it was reasonably sure that the sweating, struggling, swearing thing there on its noggin was not one.

McFadden pulled the sodden Santa cap he was wearing from over his eyes and, despite his concussion, knew immediately that he was half-naked and on top of a crocodile. This is the type of situation that human beings are evolutionarily programmed to recognize in an instant; it's just that most never get the opportunity. McFadden froze and gave the crocodile a look which, in the universal language of all living things, said 'sorry?' The crocodile retuned a look which, in the universal language of all living things, said 'at this point, with me chums looking, I'm pretty much honor bound to kill you'.

The croc opened its teeth-lined jaws and McFadden jumped up, running while still in the air, until his feet hit the sandy bank of the river and he was off like a shot, the croc in hot pursuit. Luckily, McFadden had forgotten that crocodiles can run at speeds of 10 miles per hour. Not that it mattered. The crocodile, in some higher area of lizard brain, become conscious of the fact that its pals were still watching and that not being able to kill this grimy, shrieking red animal with its skinny legs a-pumping and its tiny parts a-flapping was far less embarrassing than actually chasing it up the river. Besides, whatever it was, it was *fast*.

Almost out of breath, from a mile of running like an Olympian and squealing like a school girl, McFadden chanced a look over his shoulder. When he saw no crocodile, he slowed to a sprint and then to a hard run and then to a jog. At the exact same moment the victorious grin reached the corners of

McFadden's mouth, his father-in-law sailed into view around a bend on the river ahead.

McFadden's first thought was that they had managed to load an entirely irrational amount of unreasonably armed tribal warriors onto such a small canoe. With all of the bows and arrows and spears it looked like an oddly oversized porcupine floating towards him.

His second thought was to jump up and down, punching the air between himself and the boat, screaming British words like 'prat'.

His third thought was to run.

As they watched him go, the man next to McFadden's father-in-law turned and said, "Was that him, Chief?" It was one of those languages with clicks in.

'No," McFadden's father-in-law said, "that was an entirely different white man in a red fur suit." It was one of those answers with sarcasm in it. He pointed towards the screeching, quickly receding devil his daughter had accidentally brought home from the Outside World and the other warriors started paddling again.

Up the river the crocodile lay on the river bank, trying to sun itself. Its mates lay to the left and right, conspicuously silent. It was kind of silence required when closely watching a humiliated friend in order to see how long they would try to act as if nothing had happened. Also, crocodiles can't speak.

Suddenly, in the distance, came a low, familiar shriek growing louder as it got closer. Not quite as loud or close as the silence from the crocodile's chums, which he did his best to ignore. If crocodiles *could* speak, this one would have said,

118

"What?" He would have said it quite peevishly, too.

If crocodiles could speak, his mates would have answered, "Oh, nothing. It's just, you know, sounds like that weird screamy thing is coming back this way."

"What weird screamy thing?"

"That weird screamy thing that landed on your head awhile back."

"I'm sure I have no idea what you're talking about."

"You don't? Because I could swear that about fifteen minutes ago a weird pink and red screamy thing fell out of the jungle onto your head. And, if my eyes didn't deceive me, you chased said weird screamy thing. Furthermore, if I'm not hallucinating due to the heat, mind you, it got away. You saw it, too, din't you Brian?"

"Oh, I sure did, Harv. I remember it had flappy parts."

"See? Brian remembers it, too."

"Oh, piss off."

In the time it took that entire conversation not to happen, McFadden had burst around the corner and run past them with only a small detour up into the jungle to avoid stepping directly into three open crocodile mouths. Unfortunately, his detour took him directly into a billion-ant protest march who had come looking for revenge after finding their comrades half way down the ravine, battered and traumatized, among the ruins of a pair of shredded furry red trousers. When McFadden emerged back onto the river bank, he looked as if he were now wearing a pair of furry *black* trousers. The crocs watched all of this happen. After a pause, the one in the middle didn't say,

"Oh. *That* screamy thing."

"Why was it juggling its flappy parts, Harv?"

"Sadly, Brian, we may never know. Unless, of course, someone was to, say, catch it."

The one in the middle did, in fact, roll its eyes and start off after the ant-covered McFadden. Brian and Harv followed just in case anything else mortifying happened.

McFadden's father-in-law and *his* chums weren't close enough to start shooting arrows again but they were right behind the crocodiles. The warriors paddled furiously.

McFadden's father-in-law stood in the bow of the tiny canoe, shoulders set heroically, raven black hair blowing back majestically in the wind, eyes like chips of ancient flint gazing intently towards his rendezvous with epic destiny. Like a great battle-scarred jungle cat he leaned forward, tracking his prey, sniffing the air.

"Did you just fart?" he said and looked down at the man next to him.

The man looked up from dipping the pointy bit of an arrow into a small pot of brown sludge, "No, why?"

"What the hell are you doing?" McFadden's father-in-law said, indicating the arrow and pot.

"Oh, this? I'm dipping the pointy bit of my arrows into this pot of my own feces."

McFadden's father-in-law said, "Pointy bit?"

"Yeah. Can never remember what that part is..."

120

"Arrowhead. It's called an arrowhead. What kind of a retard can't remember that?"

"Well, now, Chief, I'm..."

"Why?"

"What?"

"Why are you dipping an arrowhead in shit?"

The man shrugged, "Just something I heard people do in this part of the world, Chief."

"People from this part of the world? You're from this part of the world. Have you ever seen anyone saving up their bowel movements in little pots for any reason whatsoever? And how did you get it all in there to begin with?"

"Well, you see, Chief..."

McFadden's father-in-law said, "If you coat your arrows in shit then you get shit in whatever you shoot. How are you going to eat something that has an infected shit-wound? That's just disgusting, now isn't it?"

"We're going to eat the red devil, then, Chief?"

McFadden's father-in-law said slowly, "Throw that pot in the river before I throw you in the river."

The splash and ripples from the pot faded quickly into the distance as the warriors paddled on.

With the exception of the four or five warthogs now chasing him, the only one McFadden had ever seen had been in that Disney movie and had seemed pleasant enough. The ones behind him were assholes. Every so often one of them would catch up to McFadden and gouge him in the ass with its things. The big, sharp, tooth-like things growing out of its mouth. The pointy bits. Mouth-horns? That didn't sound right.

McFadden had a pretty good idea that the warthogs were actually just running from the crocodiles and were trying to get past him on the narrow stretch of river bank they were all sprinting along. But he wasn't in the mood to be understanding. With his Santa hat falling over his eyes and the warthogs stabbing at his bum, any sort of compassion was completely out of the question.

To make matters worse, when McFadden and the crocs had come by, the warthogs had been drinking at a spot in the river next to a nest of some sort. McFadden wanted to say they were bees but he was relatively sure bees shouldn't be so large that you could see their claws. Or that bees had claws, for that matter.

Regardless, they hadn't taken kindly to their nest being knocked over by the warthogs trying to get out of the way of the crocodiles who were chasing McFadden who was running from his pissed-off father-in-law. The giant bees, with that uncanny bee-sense that they did entire shows about on the nature channel, had correctly decided that the skinny-legged, screaming mess in the red fur coat and hat was the cause of all of their consternation and were doing their best to jab him with *their* pointy bits.

The fact that all of the fuss had attracted a tribe of baboons was, in and of itself, neutral in the grand scheme of things. The fact that they had all identified the ant-covered McFadden as some kind of fast-moving, shrieking desert cart was a mixed blessing. Having the baboons running alongside, sometimes hanging on him, picking the biting ants off was good thing. But it meant his naughty parts were getting pinched like no one's business.

None of it, the jabbing, stinging, pinching or even the arrows that had started to land around him, now that his father-in-law had caught up to the chase, could take McFadden's mind off of the waterfall. He had started to hear it a ways back along the river, a low thrumming susurrus which he had at first attributed to inner-ear damage from being slapped in the side of the head by one of the smaller baboons who had taken up residence on his left shoulder. Soon enough he noticed the flow of the river quickening and realized there was a waterfall ahead. A huge one, by the sound of it.

Now he couldn't hear anything *but* the crash and spray of the water going over the edge of the falls. Like he would be also, momentarily. There was no question that was his fate. It was either that or stopping and becoming dead in the wet sand with an arrow through his head, gnawed on by crocodiles, trampled and crapped on by panicked warthogs, stung by giant bees, while a tribe of baboons picked ants off of his dingus. Which was not the way for a dignified gentleman such as himself to wind up. It just wasn't.

So when McFadden finally came to the waterfall he jumped. He leapt high and long in defiance of gravity and fate. Time itself seemed to slow down as he sailed forth into the mist and rainbows, flappy parts blowing back majestically in the wind. The crowd of baboons stopped at the edge of the falls, throwing themselves every which way to avoid being carried over so that, viewed as a tableau vivant, it appeared McFadden was Man bursting forth from his Primal Roots into the welcoming arms of God Himself.

The warthogs leapt, too, but all five of them plummeted like stones immediately after their hooves left the ground.

The crocodiles Harv and Brian (not their real names) were paying too much attention to see if their friend would be humiliated again and, unlike him, failed to see the waterfall until it was too late. Over they went. The croc in the middle didn't laugh and most assuredly didn't say "fuck them" before turning around and heading back to where this had all started.

Half of the tribal warriors were paddling backwards as fast as they could. McFadden's father-in-law and the men closest to him, however, were shooting arrows as fast as *they* could, hoping to spear McFadden mid-flight. One went into his thigh in roughly the same spot as the one he had pulled out some time ago. The rest of them pinged harmlessly off of the side of the helicopter. A couple of them left brown smudges.

The man next to McFadden's father-in-law shrugged sheepishly into the glare of disapproval, "I had a few already made up, Chief."

McFadden, at the apex of his leap, sailed into the open side of the helicopter which had risen up from beyond the waterfall and into the arms of his wife and a few men he assumed were forest rangers of some sort. Two of these men immediately placed McFadden on his back and began medical assistance.

One plucked the little baboon off of McFadden's shoulder and, after verifying that McFadden didn't want to keep it, tossed the little primate out of the helicopter. It dropped into the crashing waterfall, making a disappearing sound quite similar to the *'wheeee!'* of humans on circus rides until it was speared mid-tumble by an arrow and fell silently out of sight.

The last man pointed a rifle at McFadden's father-in-law but gave him a look which, in the universal language of men who kill things, said 'nice shot'. McFadden's father-in-law returned a look which, in the universal language of men who kill things, said 'I was trying to hit *you*'.

McFadden's wife, after checking to make sure he wasn't dead, stepped into the door of the helicopter with a bullhorn she had procured from somewhere. She put it to her mouth to address her father and there were so many rapid-fire clicks and whirs that McFadden couldn't tell if his wife was just really angry or if the bullhorn was malfunctioning. Either way she seemed to have made her point as McFadden's father-in-law and the rest of the tribal warriors reluctantly put down their bows and arrows, turned around and paddled back up the river. Then she was back, hovering above him as the helicopter flew away from the waterfall and, McFadden hoped, towards whiskey.

"Tony!" she said with the accent on the syllable which didn't exist. She pronounced his name as if she were cataloguing parts of his leg from the ground up, "My sweet Tony!"

"Umlele!" McFadden wheezed, "My dear, beloved Umlele!"

She leaned closer, "Yes, my Tony?"

"Umlele!"

Closer. "Yes, Tony?"

McFadden sat straight up. "WHAT THE FUCK JUST HAPPENED?" One of the medics pushed him gently back down.

Umlele frowned. "Well what the fuck were you doing dressing up like Father Christman anyway, Tony? In the middle of the jungle, no less."

"It's Father *Christmas*, dear. I was dressed up as Father Christmas. I thought it would be a good way to break the ice since it is, in fact, fucking Christmas."

"Well, whatever. They don't even celebrate the Christmas. To them you looked like the Red Devil from the tribal legends."

"You mean to tell me that they chased me across half of the God forsaken jungle and shot me with shit-covered arrows all because they thought I was a monster?" McFadden said.

"No, they knew you were only dressed up as the monster. They chased you because my father is the Chief and he chased you because he wanted to kill you for having the sex with his daughter without his permission. That is the way people do things in this part of the world. And who covers their arrows in shit? That is disgusting." Umlele said, "And what means this 'Ho Ho Ho'? Because, in our language, it means 'I have come to violate the skulls of your dead children'. I think that may also have had something to do with all of the chasing and the shooting of arrows."

"I have no pants on," McFadden observed sadly.

"Yes, Tony. I know this," Umlele said and gently patted his arm.

"Umlele?" McFadden said.

"Yes, my beloved Tony?"

"Next year? We're spending Christmas with my family."

126

'Conscription Fit'

by Val Tenterhosen

"Ya ain't supposed ta *eat it*," Marge said, running up and hastily shutting off the hose.

"You cream corn, this is what you get," replied Georgina, her even more po-dunky sister. "You get creamed goddamn corn, I tell you what."

"No more of that sass!"

Marge slapped Georgina across the face.

"Lepers and leprechauns is all you're good at." She was blinking back tears, but sounded defiant.

Marge slapped her again. Harder.

"You couldn't fart in a barrel if someone stuffed you into one, Marge. You're nothing but a pile of dried farts, is all you are."

Marge slapped her a third time. Her wiry sister crumpled to the ground.

"I'm going to grind you up and feed you to pigs," Marge said, her breath heaving. She wiped the sweat off her upper lip with a dirty thumb. Mud smeared her face. "I'm going to dunk you in outhouse droppings and leave you to rot in the sun."

Georgina didn't get up.

"You get on up and fight me like a man!" Marge cried,

suddenly acutely aware of the oppressive noon heat. Her unwashed sundress was soaked through. "You get up, you cowardly shit!"

Georgina didn't take orders.

Marge stood there, trembling, until she saw red ants climbing into Georgina's ears. Her sister, sprawled face down on the dry earth, did nothing to shoo them away.

Marge began to scream.

'Death of a Phobia:
Pugwash plus 2 and the Pasty-faced Fuckers'

by David Eccles

"Alright, who's the clever cunt, drawing pictures of dicks on the table tops again?"

Jason Malbon, manager of *The Unique Horn* rock and metal bar scanned the sea of silent faces staring back at him, in the hope that he could spot the flushed cheeks of the person responsible. However, the culprit remained unfound.

Somebody, somewhere in the bar farted, and the uncomfortable silence was broken, replaced by raucous laughter and the sound of clinking beer glasses.

"This puerile shit's got to stop," Jason shouted, throwing down a solvent-soaked rag and wiping the sweat from his brow on his rolled up shirt sleeve. "I mean it, guys. I'm getting sick and fucking tired of cleaning up after the whole lot of you. You could at least use something that's easy to clean off instead of using that permanent marker shit. And," he warned, "whoever it was that squeezed out that fart, I hope you bought a spare pair of pants, 'cause that fucker sounded *wet!*"

He stowed the can of solvent and the cleaning cloth under the counter and left the bar unattended so that he could patrol the joint and collect dirty glasses as he went, all the while keeping an eye open for anyone using a permanent marker pen.

"And just what are you miscreants plotting now?" Jason

collected and stacked the empty pint glasses littering the table nearest to the bar, his attention focused mainly on Drew Edmunds, a blond-haired, blue-eyed misfit who was idly doodling in a notebook with a ballpoint. He scowled and gritted his teeth, noticing yet another pictorial penis had been penned on the table top directly in front of where Drew sat.

"Not much, dude, and before you accuse me of anything, it wasn't me who drew that. My pen's blue." Drew offered Jason his best fake smile. "We're just thinking about going to the circus that's pitched a tent down by the park, but *this* ballbag is shit-scared of clowns and won't go with us." Drew made a stabbing gesture with his pen, indicating Pugwash, a farmer's son, who had left behind his tractor, moved to the city and adopted a lifestyle of facial piercings, strong beer, fast food, and heavy metal music.

Pugwash shivered upon hearing the C-word. "Did you have to say it?" He threw a salted cashew nut at Drew, who caught it and tossed it into his mouth with a flourish.

"See that? I'm a fucking ninja!" he joked, winking at Pugwash.

"You're a fucking dick is what you are! You know I suffer from coulrophobia. I don't just dislike clowns; I'm scared to death of the pasty-faced fuckers! They give me the creeps."

Jason stared in disbelief at the long-haired, bearded giant of a man cowering before him, a nervous wreck just because Drew had uttered the word that Pugwash dreaded. "Would it help if you thought of the word spelled with a K instead of a C, dude?"

Pugwash squealed like a pig. "Jason, that's not funny. In fact, it's worse. I can't even watch that movie or even look at a picture of a... you know what."

130

"I'm just trying to help, dude. Maybe you should get some professional help with that, 'cause how else are you going to manage if you suddenly fancy buying a Happy Meal from Maccy D's?" Jason winked at Alicia before moving away from the group to finish collecting his glasses, a signal that he was handing the Pugwash-teasing baton over to her.

"Very funny... *not,*" complained Pugwash, taking an enormous swig of beer before slamming his glass down on the table.

"And I thought I was supposed to be the girl, you wuss." Alicia poked him in the gut with a well-manicured finger, and then groped at his expansive chest. "You scream like a girl when you see a clown, and you've even got bigger tits than me!"

In response to her teasing, Pugwash prodded her left breast. She quickly slapped his hand away. "Hey, no fair," he complained. "Your lot, meaning women in general, wanted sexual equality, so if you're going to feel my tits, I reserve the right to feel yours. Well, what little there is to feel, anyway," he retorted, in jest.

"Fuck off, fat boy!" She snapped, feigning hurt before playfully elbowing him in the ribs. He grunted, then threw his arms around her in a huge bear hug and kissed her forehead.

"Aw, you love me really," he joked. "And just so you know, there's nothing wrong with your tits, Alicia. They're really nice, actually. I've seen the photos online."

"Hey, those photographs are purely artistic. I am a model, after all," she stated with pride. "There's nothing at all sexual about those images."

"Oh, I wouldn't say that," said Drew, grinning as he closed his notebook. "I've enjoyed a good wank over your tits on more than one occasion. Figuratively speaking, of course," he added, stroking his D'Artagnan moustache and beard.

Alicia gave him her best fake smile. "You're such a dirty bastard."

Drew held up his hands. "Hey, it was meant as a compliment. I'm very choosy who I wank over, I'll have you know."

"Well, in that case, thanks... I think."

"The pleasure's all mine," he said, winking.

Pugwash's huge fist pounded the table, and his two friends recoiled in shock.

"Fuck, bro, you frightened the life out of me!" Drew took a few deep breaths to calm his nerves. "What's up with you?"

"I'm going to do it."

"Do what?"

"I'm coming with the two of you — to the circus. I figure I'll have to conquer this irrational fear sooner or later, and, as the circus is in town, there's no time like the present. Shall we go?"

Alicia hugged Pugwash, kissed his cheek and whispered in his ear. "I'm very proud of you, Tim. Let's go kick some clown ass, yeah?"

He stiffened as soon as she mentioned the C-word, and then relaxed once more, realizing that Alicia had used his given first name instead of his nickname. It felt good. "Let's do this. You

132

ready, Drew?"

"Nearly, dude. Just give me a second or two, bro." Making doubly sure that no one was watching, Drew took a miniature Sharpie from his pants pocket and drew spurts of ejaculate above the cartoon cock that decorated the table top. Admiring his artwork, he pocketed his pen, got up from the table and left the bar, with Pugwash and Alicia grinning broadly as they followed in his wake.

* * *

"Well, here we are, dude and dudette," said Drew, both arms stretched wide. "I present to you the greatest show on earth: Caligari's Circus!"

Alicia was wide-eyed and grinning like a Cheshire Cat. She clapped her hands and jumped up and down in pure excitement. Pugwash snorted; Alicia's actions reminded him of a demented sea lion after it had performed a trick.

"It looks like a bunch of barbers have all gone camping together in a massive red and white striped, minty-looking tent," he said, clearly unimpressed. Alicia elbowed Pugwash in the ribs.

"Don't spoil it for me, Tim. This is a first for me. I've never been to a circus before."

"That makes two of us, Alicia," croaked Pugwash, nursing his bruised ribcage. "Drew? How about you? Have you been to a circus before?"

Drew took a long pull on the cigarette he had just lit then held it in front of his mouth. He blew on the tip, watching it intently as the glow changed from a deep red to a bright orange and a steady stream of smoke escaped from his lips. "Yeah, I've been to a circus before, but not since I was a kid. There used to be lots of animal acts in those days, but they changed the law so that circuses couldn't use 'em anymore and that put most circuses out of business. A lot of animals had to be put to sleep too, 'cause they couldn't find suitable homes for all of them. It's a damn shame." He flicked his cigarette and watched its arc until the glowing tip landed in a nearby puddle of water and was extinguished.

Pugwash nodded in approval. "Good shot, dude."

"Hey, what can I say, bro? It's all down to the ninja training." Drew flashed a smile and winked at Alicia, then spun on his heels to perform a high-level karate block and a punch to the solar plexus of an invisible opponent before strutting over to the box office.

"Just look at him, Tim," Alicia giggled. "Six months of karate training at the YMCA and now he thinks he's Chuck Norris. We'd better catch up with him before he trips over his own shadow! "

By the time Pugwash and Alicia caught up with Drew, he had already paid their admission fee and pocketed their tickets and had struck up a conversation with the occupant of the box office, a man who, Pugwash thought, bore a disturbing resemblance to both Malcolm MacDowell's Alex in *A Clockwork Orange* and Liza Minnelli's character Sally Bowles in *Cabaret*.

He shuddered at the thought that the guy might be wearing a waistcoat, stockings, garter belt, jazz pants and tap shoes behind the counter, and craned his neck to confirm if this was indeed the case. The kohl eyeliner, false eyelash attached to his left eyelid and the crudely applied bright red lipstick was deeply unsettling, as was the Bowler hat, but Pugwash stood firm, determined to beat his phobia of all things remotely clown-like.

"Our family is committed to the pursuit of excellence, and making sure that all who witness our show have the most unforgettable time of their lives," boasted the box office attendant in what Pugwash deemed to be a well-rehearsed speech, though he had to admit, it was delivered with the utmost passion. "We are a very proud family, with a strong sense of tradition deeply rooted in history, and the Big Top is our home. It shapes who we are, defines us. Without it, we are nothing."

"Aw, that was very moving," sighed Alicia. "That's an interesting accent, by the way. Where are your family from, originally?"

"Thank you, dear lady," said the box office attendant, tipping his Bowler hat. "Please allow me to introduce myself. My name is Alessandro Caligari, and my family's origins lie in the south of Italy, and quite possibly, Greece. In Latin, the family name means 'shoemaker,' but I much prefer the translation derived from the Greek words 'cale' which means 'beautiful' and 'jaris' which means 'grace.' It is a much more fitting translation, as you will see when the show begins." He smiled at Alicia, who blushed at the olive-skinned man's attention.

"Cheers, dude," said Pugwash, grabbing Alicia by the arm and pulling her towards the Big Top.

"Did you see how he looked at you then, Alicia?" he whispered.

"I know," sighed Alicia. "Alessandro has a lovely smile, don't you think?"

"No, I don't," snapped Pugwash. "In fact, I'd say that was definitely a leer, not a smile."

"You're right, bro. That was definitely a leer," agreed Drew, his facial expression suddenly serious for once.

Drew buried both hands in the pockets of his leather trenchcoat and strode towards the Big Top, mindful of the flickering light bulbs adorning the entrance. He told himself that it was just the generators acting up, but the uneasy feeling in the pit of his stomach remained.

* * *

Drew leaned forward in his seat, annoyed by Pugwash's constant squirming. "Dude, will you keep fucking still!"

"Leave him alone, Drew! Can't you see he's nervous?" hissed Alicia.

"I can't help it, bro. This seat's making my ass numb!" said Pugwash in hushed tones.

"Guys, stop talking around my tits!" Alicia gave them both a firm elbow to the mid-section.

"I'm just trying to keep abreast of the situation." Drew grinned, satisfied with his attempt at humour, especially as it drew a snort from Pugwash.

"Drew, watch your fucking language! There are kids in the audience," warned Alicia, completely unaware of the F-bomb she herself had just dropped.

A loud gurgling sound caught the attention of both Drew and Alicia who swiveled in their seats, curious to discover the source of the noise. "Sorry, guys. I can't help feeling hungry."

Pugwash patted his belly. "Anyone fancy some popcorn?" He paused for a beat, awaiting a reply, and both Drew and Alicia shook their heads. "Okay, your loss. Drew, lend me your Sharpie before I go." Drew handed over the marker pen, curious as to what Pugwash wanted with it, but Pugwash was gone before Drew could ask.

By the time Pugwash returned, the Big Top was full, and the chatter of the audience had grown to a dull roar. Small groups of children dotted around the ring shrieked with joy, and the odd one or two could be heard crying, either because they were tired and wanted to go home already or because they had been chastised by their parents for being too rowdy and vociferous.

In a split-second, the lights went out, which elicited a shriek from the majority of the female members of the audience, though Pugwash himself screeched like a parrot at being plunged into sudden darkness.

"Fucking wuss," said Drew and Alicia in unison, which drew a laugh from a few members of the surrounding audience. Pugwash shrank into his seat, clearly embarrassed, but he continued stuffing popcorn into his sizable mouth, getting butter all over his beard in the process.

A spotlight lit up the center of the ring, a plume of white smoke mushroomed, and a resounding crash of thunder filled the Big Top, resulting in *"Oohs"* and *"Aahs"* from the crowd. The acrid smell of gunpowder filled the air and, as the smoke began to clear, the tall, majestic figure of the Ringmaster slowly materialized, wearing the traditional uniform of scarlet tails jacket with gold filigree, white riding breeches, black riding boots, top hat and white gloves.

"Ladies and Gentlemen, Children of all Ages. On behalf of Circus Caligari, I welcome you, one and all to the Greatest

Show on Earth!" The Ringmaster gave an eloquent opening speech, sprinkled with a liberal dusting of hyperbole and excellent examples of alliteration, much to the delight of the audience. The public address system delivered a rousing rendition of Fucik's *March of the Gladiators* and the whole company of performers completed a few laps of the ring before disappearing once more to finalize preparations for their individual acts.

The finale of the opening ceremony gave rise to rapturous applause and much cheering from the audience, which was graciously acknowledged by The Ringmaster who took a bow and without further ado announced the first act, Ekaterina Kim, an aerial specialist who was making a guest appearance for that night only.

The spotlight swung away from the Ringmaster to highlight the base of the tower used by the aerial performers to climb to their assigned platform, but instead of the sequined, Russian beauty the crowd expected to see, the harsh glare of the super trouper illuminated the grotesque figure of a hunchback in full whiteface make-up and dressed as a Harlequin hauling himself up to the staging platform with what appeared to be a stiletto blade between his teeth and a murderous glint in his eyes. Chase music like that played by pit orchestras in the golden age of silent movies blared out of the public address system, accompanying the twisted clown as he climbed and a second spotlight lit the darkness high above the ground to reveal the Russian aerial artiste, whose only possible means of escape from certain death at the hands of the crazed clown was to jump and risk almost-certain death upon impact with the sawdust-covered ground far below.

Pugwash watched on, open-mouthed in horrified paralysis and Alicia screamed, digging her fingernails into the thighs of both Pugwash and Drew, who bore a huge grin. One of Alicia's acrylic nails snapped off due to the intensity of her fear-induced grip, but Alicia failed to notice. "Oh my god," she shrieked. "Somebody help her!"

"This is so fucking cool!" said Drew, giggling in his mania. "It's like the Cirque du Soleil, but better!"

The sensation of Alicia's fingers digging into the meat of his thigh wrenched Pugwash out of his reverie and he winced, biting his lip as he prised her hand from his leg. "I fucking *knew* it was a bad idea coming here tonight. I could *feel* it in the pit of my stomach."

All around the trio — who remained seated — children screamed hysterically. They dropped their drinks, their popcorn and their cotton candy; a large number of them lost control of their bowels and evacuated their bladders, and the Big Top soon began to reek of shit and piss. Parents scrambled towards the Big Top exit, dragging their kids behind them while carrying the younger ones in their arms, desperately trying to shield their innocent eyes and prevent them from witnessing the unspeakable horror of what was about to happen. A few unfortunate souls were trampled underfoot and lost their lives in the confusion and chaos.

High above the screaming horde, the hunchbacked Harlequin hauled himself up onto the aerial platform, took the stiletto blade from between his teeth and, grinning from ear to ear, swung at the Russian artiste in a sideways slashing motion. She screamed and drew in her abdomen at the last moment, narrowly avoiding the blade before launching herself backwards into the air like an Olympic ten-metre platform diver.

Pugwash, Drew and Alicia watched in amazement as the Russian somersaulted during her descent, decelerated rapidly as she neared the ground and landed as light as a feather before vaulting skyward again and completing yet more advanced acrobatic manoeuvres.

"Man, that's fucking brilliant!" shouted Drew. "She's using rebound straps, and they're invisible! Well, not invisible, but… you know what I mean, dude. I knew it was all just a part of the act," he lied.

"Hmmm." Pugwash's attention remained fixed on the clown, who appeared to be extremely incensed by the "escape" of his intended victim and was growling and gnashing his teeth as he hung on to a support wire, trying his damnedest to rip into the flesh of Ekaterina Kim as she catapulted towards him.

Alicia held her head in her hands and peered out from between spread fingers. "Drew, I don't think this is a part of the show. Have you seen the look on its face? That's not a man, it's a fucking monster!"

Remembering the uneasy feeling he'd experienced earlier, Drew cast his eyes around the Big Top and it at once dawned on him that in only a couple of minutes the whole tent had been evacuated and that now he, Pugwash and Alicia were all that remained of the audience, and although the only sounds of screaming came from Ekaterina Kim, the music from the public address system had a dissonant quality that was, in equal parts, nerve-shattering and an all-out assault on the senses.

"I want to get out of here, boys. I want to go now!" sobbed Alicia. "Something really bad's going to happen, and I don't want to be here when it does." She threw her arms around Pugwash and buried her face in his chest. "Take me home, Tim."

"I think it's a little late for that, Alicia," said Pugwash matter-of-factly, his normally expressive voice completely devoid of emotion.

It happened so fast, in the same time-frame that Alicia was pleading to be whisked away to safety. Timing his jump to perfection, the knife-wielding, chequered abomination launched from the aerial platform, collided with Ekaterina Kim and knocked the wind out of her. He clung to her back and rode her unconscious form down to the ground, the weight of his horrifyingly abnormal musculature overpowering the elasticity of the rebound straps.

Treating her as he would a piece of meat, the Harlequin threw Ekaterina onto her back and tore open her throat with his blade, clapping his hands with glee as he watched her lifeblood spurt from the gaping wound in her neck in an ever-diminishing arc. He raised his knife once more, plunged it deep into her belly, and dragged it down with enough force to cut through both costume and flesh and make a hole large enough to accommodate his huge hands which, after dropping the blade, he then forced into the grisly pocket he had just created.

As a warped finale to this "opening act" the Harlequin pulled out Ekaterina's intestines and, accompanied by a drumroll and a fanfare of trumpets from the public address speakers, he sprang clear of her body and the rebound straps took her corpse up into the air once more. The terrible figure of the Harlequin stood beneath the dripping, bouncing corpse wearing a maniacal grin and holding a handful of intestines which remained attached to the body and, for a brief moment, it reminded Pugwash of someone holding a helium balloon.

The Ringmaster strode out into the center of the ring, followed closely by four diminutive clowns who ran around whooping and hollering with delight as they dipped their white-gloved hands into the pooled blood and licked their fingers. "Hungry!" they crowed in unison.

"Patience, little ones," crooned the Ringmaster, motioning for the greasepainted ghouls to be calm. "It is not yet feeding time and, if you hadn't noticed, we still have a few... *guests* to entertain."

Harlequin released his grip on the intestinal "balloon string" and, motioning towards Pugwash, Drew and Alicia, he barked a few guttural orders in a language never before heard by human ears. All four clowns turned their gaze towards the trio and they began to fan out as they slowly inched their way forward with eyes blazing and lips drawn back, exposing a double row of razor-sharp teeth.

"Fuck this, dude!" said Drew. "I don't fancy getting eaten alive by evil midget clowns in really bad wigs!"

"I'm with you there, bro. Come on, Alicia. Let's get out of here before Pennywise's progeny sink their teeth in our asses!" Pugwash was on his feet before Alicia had even opened her mouth to reply and, pausing briefly to rub his numb ass and get the blood flowing again, he picked Alicia up and ran with her under his arm towards the Big Top exit, making sure that Drew was hot on their heels.

They had gone no more than thirty feet when the silhouette of a man wearing a Bowler hat and gripping a baseball bat barred their way.

"Alessandro!" gasped Alicia. "Leave him to me, Tim. I'll sort this."

"You'd better, and fast, Alicia. Use your feminine wiles. That always seems to work," Pugwash joked feebly.

He set her down, and Alicia thanked him then took a deep

controlled breath, exhaled, exhibiting the same level of control and marched up to the man who earlier that evening had made her go weak at the knees. Their eyes met, only this time she felt not weakness but an adrenaline-fuelled strength coursing through her body. "Get out of my way, you fucking freak!"

"I'm afraid that's not possible, dear lady," Alessandro shrugged. "We have so many more delights for you and your two friends to experience and, as they say, the show must go on." His grip tightened on the baseball bat angled over his shoulder, and his wide grin revealed that he bore the same piranha-like dentition as the other clowns.

Alicia shook her head, unfazed by his ghoulish implication. "Nah, the curtain's coming down on tonight's performance."

With lightning speed, she drove her right knee into the clown's groin, causing him to lose his grip on the baseball bat and sink to his knees. He cupped his crushed testicles while vomiting small chunks of what Alicia could only assume was human flesh.

"I'll take this, if you don't mind." She snatched the Bowler hat from Alessandro's head and tried it on for size. "Perfect," she said, tilting the Bowler and flicking the brim. "Come on, boys."

"Ooh, I felt that, dude." Pugwash drew a sharp breath and patted Alessandro on the shoulder before stepping around him and joining Alicia outside the Big Top.

Drew shook his head in disbelief. "Man, who'd have thought it? Evil clowns have balls! Well, apart from you, bro. Ha!" He picked up the baseball bat and took a few practice swings, nodded with satisfaction at its performance. "And *I'll* take this, thank you very much. There's no point in you owning a bat if you don't have any balls!" He sidestepped the puking Pierrot and began making his way towards the exit.

He took a quick glance over his shoulder towards the ring, and at that very moment all thoughts of personal safety left his mind and the full horror of what he and his two friends had witnessed began to sink in. People have lost their lives tonight, he thought, and not in the usual way one generally thinks of when hearing about someone dying. They hadn't lost their lives in a car crash, and they hadn't succumbed to smoke inhalation in a burning building. These people had died in a manner that he'd only ever read about in books or seen in movies. Their broken, trampled bodies still lay where they had fallen and were by now being feasted on by those … things. Drew shuddered at the thought of how Ekaterina Kim had died, and he hoped that she had been unconscious and hadn't suffered as the Harlequin's knife ripped her apart.

"Bro, I need you with me. Come on, dude. Snap out of it!" Pugwash roared.

Drew turned to his friend, a mixture of both sadness and rage showing in his eyes and in his body language. Pugwash knew instinctively what Drew was thinking. "It's okay, bro. No need to say it. Alicia was right when she said those things were monsters."

Drew looked around, seeking out Alicia who was nowhere to be seen. "Where is she anyway, bro? I don't see her anywhere."

"Calm it, dude. I sent her on an errand. She'll be back in a second or two, you'll see."

As if on cue, Alicia emerged from the darkness, struggling with a metal jerry can filled with a liquid that sloshed around as she walked. "I think I found some, Tim. It was next to one of the generators, on the back of a pickup truck. I hope it's what you were after." She dumped the jerry can at Pugwash's feet and stood hands-on-hips, breathing heavily from her exertions.

Pugwash got down on his haunches, unscrewed the top of the can, sniffed, and nodded. "It's perfect for what I have in mind, Alicia."

Drew's face lit up. "Are we having a barbecue?"

"One could say that, dude," Pugwash grinned. "I remembered something Alessandro said about the Big Top defining who they are. He said that without it, they're nothing. You've seen enough horror movies, bro. What's the most common way to get rid of monsters?"

"Kill it, with fire!" Drew and Alicia chanted in unison.

"Damn right!" Pugwash nodded in agreement. "Let's cook these pasty-faced fuckers!"

* * *

Alicia played tic-tac-toe by herself, writing in the condensation on the window of the busy diner while Pugwash and Drew sat opposite her, deep in conversation.

"It's been a week, bro and there's been nothing in the newspapers or on the TV. I just don't understand it. We watched that tent burn, heard the screams those things made as they turned crispy." Pugwash added more sugar to his cup and stirred his tea.

"I know, bro," said Drew. "There was something I read in the local rag, but that was about an illegal rave. It said dozens of people had reported seeing a murder being committed, but the authorities blamed it all on mass hysteria and drug-induced psychosis. They said the reports had probably all been phoned in by people who had been to the rave and who had drunk bottles of water laced with Ecstasy. Can you believe that?"

Pugwash took a sip of his tea. "No, that's bullshit, man. There were small kids there, and they don't do drugs or raves. It's definitely been covered up. There are people dead. Somebody must have reported family members missing, surely."

"I'm with you, bro. I'm betting there's some kind of secret government department that deals with this kind of stuff, hushing it up as it happens." Drew shuddered. "I find that way scarier than any clown ever could be. Do you know, sometimes I even wonder if it ever happened at all."

"Oh, it happened, alright, guys," said Alicia, wiping the condensation from her hands with a paper napkin. "I really did wonder if it was all just a delusion, too, so I went back the very next day and I found… this."

Reaching into her bag, she pulled out a slightly singed, ragged piece of heavy red and white canvas. "That could have come from anywhere, Alicia," said Drew. "It doesn't prove there was ever a circus or that we were even there if there was a circus."

Pugwash choked, spitting tea. "Fuck, I'd forgotten about that."

"Forgotten about what?" said Drew, puzzled.

Alicia unfolded the canvas and laid it out on the table.

"Dude! *That's* why you wanted to borrow my Sharpie!"

146

Drew howled with laughter.

"Yeah, bro. I needed yours 'cause mine had run dry," said Pugwash.

There, scrawled across the canvas in permanent black ink was a drawing of a huge cock.

Pugwash grinned. "You're not the only artist at this table, bro."

'Sentinel'

by John Boden

Sitting here in this chair again. It isn't comfortable. An old under-stuffed antique chair, purchased for eye appeal rather than practicality. It sits along the wall at the top of the steps. I sit here when the journey from bathroom to kitchen becomes too much.

I was sick.

Was, I say, as if one is ever not sick. We die every day in a thousand ways. A thousand cancers painted like words or deeds. We hide them under scarves and shirts or jackets and suits. Well-scrubbed skin and sculpted hair, as we fester beneath.

After my second shower, I had every inclination of going down and making a nice breakfast. But I got lightheaded and sat down for a minute. I was sitting in this very chair, perched forward and staring down to the landing.

Through the stairwell gate and dirty window pane, and over the outside decking and faded railing, I see it.

The sky has bled from blue to gray to cadaverous white. It stands at the edge of the property line. Too long arms above its large egg-shaped head. Goopy red eyes and a yawning circle rimmed with lost fingernails for teeth. A Medusa crown of used bandages and IV tubing. It wears my ratty robe, my pajamas and my slippers. Pictures of dead relatives pinned to its flesh with stick pins. It has my briefcase and my coffee thermos and my laptop, tied around its long, thin neck by braids of what was once my hair. Once on my head. A month ago, maybe weeks.

I catch myself muttering, "With my cross-bow, I shot the albatross."

* * *

Just two weeks ago, I was given the clean bill from the doctor, I rejoiced. I was better. Remission they call it, a silly name, like "Do-It-Again-Mission"... fuck that. Once was enough. All the medicine and chemicals. The sickness to beat the sickness. I got the news that I was free and clear and felt born again. I proclaimed my joys to world and spirit and family and friends. I wrote all my hateful thoughts on napkins and burned them in the kiln. The ashes swirled and mingled with the night. I turned a new leaf, hoped to walk tall and get right.

I should have known, you're never really better. Cancer, like a lie, always comes back. Better, they said. Than who, or what?

* * *

It was a simple matter of days before the sentinel showed up. Standing on the edge of all that is mine. Staring and minding the line. I was frightened before I figured it out. It's all about legacy. Inheritance.

My cancer ghost, my anger and my black made flesh. A living scarecrow of tumor and tenacity, bile and blood. It stands and marks the way, shouts the standard. I sit on this chair, at the top of the stairs and stare down, through the stairwell gate and the dirty windowpane, out over the decking to the edge of the dying yard. That is where I see it, getting closer each day. Coming for to carry me home.

'The Overly-Attached Succubus'

by M.C. O'Neill

Dedicated to Sister J. Abigail Stenman

Hues of salmon and rose tinged the blanket of mist and smog hanging in the evening sky above Westlake Village McMansion. He was worried he was going to be late for the signing, but upon seeing that the courtyard was empty, it appeared he had a leg-up on the agent.

There was something weasel-like about her, Mario feared, but then again, real estate was a shady business in this day and age. Sure, he'd signed contract after contract with publishers, and the process had more or less become rote, but buying his first house was a daunting prospect. Bottom line: he didn't want to get screwed.

For the first time since he had left for college, Mario Poon would live in an actual home. No more rattraps stacked side-by-side into brownstones earmarked for condemnation. No longer would he have to suffer "posh" studios with only one door and maybe two windows facing a brick wall. This was going to be a grand journey into *real* living.

It had taken some time, but his writing had, at last, provided a modicum of success. Mario struggled like most through the ghettos of indie publishing before graduating to small presses and, in time, he had secured his first "Big Six" deal. Once he'd hit the New York Times Bestsellers' list he could barely keep up with his ever-increasing bank balance. All in all, it was a fun ride, if not a bumpy one.

The majestic mobile home had two garages, two levels, what looked like an attic towering from somewhere near the center of its blueprint, pilasters guarding the front doors, and it boasted gables. *Fucking gables!* Never before had Mario dreamed that owning such an abode could be possible — and all atop titanic monster truck tires.

As he soaked in the luxury looming before him, the steady whine of a German import caught his attention. Candace Claren was her name. He doubted it was her real one. There was something a little too bougie about it. Perhaps it was the alliteration. It was true that practically everyone in his line of work used, and was known by, a pseudonym, but aliases were just not for Mario; they made him feel weird and fake.

As in their online meeting, her personal appearance was no less lavish. Her platinum power-bang hung to a perfect point, and she was dripping in Dolce & Gabbana and reeking of Coco. What unnerved Mario was her smile, nay, *smirk*, which must have been practiced ever since her sorority days at whatever state-run university. It was always on, as if she was having the time of her life with her clients, but it was also somehow haughty and… *sinister*?

"Yaah," she oozed, like she always would when feigning excitement. "Mario, it's so wonderful to meet with you again. It's your big day, yes?"

That voice. *Grating.* It was what really gave away her artifices. She was, possibly, a native of Wisconsin, no — Minnesota, but at some point had been trained to Californianize her diphthongs to near-charm school perfection. *What a poseur.*

He waved, if not somewhat like a shy kid. "Hi, again, Ms. Claren."

"No, no, no!" she pipped. "Please… You can call me Candace." It came out of her mouth as "Caaandace."

"Okay. *Caaandace*." He mimicked, hoping she didn't catch the rub.

Apparently she did, as she cocked a galvanized brow and huffed. "Right, then. Let's get on with the show, shall we?"

She swaggered with arrogance before him as she led him to the door. Her pretentious locomotion made her appear to hover. Mario tried to ape her movement when she wasn't looking, but he couldn't quite nail it down. This too must have been well-rehearsed over the years.

"Oh, I must tell you that my niece loves all of your books," Candace announced as they walked up the cobblestone steps. "I myself don't have children. Just don't have the time for it, really. Didn't you say they were written for homosexual teens?"

"Asexual," Mario corrected. "Asexual teens."

The agent couldn't hide the puzzled look on her face. "Yaah… *Asexual*?"

Mario made great effort to contain a roll of his eyeballs. "They're people who don't want to have sex with anyone."

Her gasp echoed under the mobile mansion's main eaves. "No sex? I never knew such a thing could exist. Well, that doesn't sound like much fun. Why, just last weekend, the girls and I went up to Fresno and… Oh, never mind. It's time for the grand tour!"

"Sounds good." He wanted to get this to-do over with, and soon. Not just to be done with the nerves of signing on to such a milestone, but to be out of the aroma of her pomp.

"Oh, and before we do enter," she said. "I just want to tell you a little something about your new neighborhood. Over to your right was once the home of Will Smith. Well, you know, before he was incinerated in that horrible filming accident."

"Yes," Mario nodded. "I heard he was set to play the new Human Torch, but the pyrotechnics or something set his head alight."

"Yaah! That's right. Up in smoke, so they say. Terrible, terrible." She pivoted on a stilettoed heel without any more thought for the doomed actor. "And over to your left is the home of musician, Kenny Loggins. I can't for the life of me remember what he recorded, but he was famous and he's your neighbor, regardless."

Mario shrugged. "I think it was the soundtrack to that golf movie that came out a long time ago. I don't remember it either, really. I was just a toddler."

"Oh!" Candace cheeped. "Do you play? We have a green not far from here, you know."

Somewhat irritated, he shook his head. Her company was making his head spin. "Can't say I do."

"Well, then let's *entre*," she said in lousy French.

Though the exterior was remarkable in design, once the French-style front doors parted, revealing the inner bowels of the new digs, Mario was treated to a display of true wonder. He could not believe that all of this was going to be his.

Masonic checkerboard tiled the floor of the main hall. Rich, dark mahogany panels gave the place a dirge of perpetual dusk. To most, the place would have appeared too dreary and Gothic, but Mario found the tones warm and rather eccentric. After all, he was well acquainted with all sorts of dismal topics, having founded the new literary movement known as "Lichpunk."

"Now this is right up my alley," he said as he absorbed the mighty opulence. The trio of immense crystal chandeliers was his favorite feature and it was quite the surprise that it was pre-furnished in rather formidable effects.

"Yaah," she drawled. "It is a lot to take in, yes? Of course, the furniture is all yours to keep, if you like; however, we can have it removed straight away if you wish."

"Oh, no!" blurted Mario. "I love it. Everything's perfect. Besides, I've recently come from well… rather meager means, so I could use the stuff. This is great!"

With heels clacking across the tiled floor, Claren ushered him deeper into the corridor. "Aw," she sympathized, her honeyed tone dripping with sarcasm. "It must have been so trifling being a starving artist, yes? Well, those days are over, my dear."

"Well, it wasn't all *that* awful, but… "

Claren cared not to hear about his Bohemian history, instead turning away and clopping further into the tour. In many ways, Mario was relieved her rudeness belayed that topic.

Marble-tiled bathrooms — three of them; a gourmet kitchen that could feed an army with its stainless-steel appliances, and four bedrooms were all endemic to the house's architecture. A small gymnasium filled with high-end Nautilus equipment and a games room lined with classic arcade models such as *Dig-*

Dug, GORF, Dragon's Lair and *Blueprint* enjoyed a home here. The library, attached to a cozy, dark den was what really impressed him, filled as it was with classics and tomes that he had always wanted to read; some of them were sure to be first editions, he hoped. It would be nothing less than a wonderful place to write. Mario was amazed that this was now his property, and after the shock and joy had subsided, a touch, a pang of paranoia kissed his brain.

"Eh, Candace?"

"Yaah?"

"This place is awesome, but why would someone want to leave all of this great stuff behind? I mean, the price of this sweet arcade alone could fetch a pretty penny."

Once again, she ignored him. "Yaah, let's not dawdle, Mario. Let's get to the main dining room and make this place officially yours, shall we?"

Once they were under the grand chandelier, they commenced the haggling. Aside from the included furnishings, Mario could not digest the low price of it all. In haste, he produced his favorite pen and signed the dotted line to the mortgage. "Yaah!" she exclaimed. "All done. Welcome to your new, not-so-humble home, Mario."

He smiled. "Thanks!"

As he ushered her toward the front door and the awaiting evening, Claren paused before finally stepping beyond the mansion's threshold. "Eh, there's one more little tidbit I must inform you of before I leave."

This is it, he thought. *Here's where I get it up the ass.*

"Yes?"

"*Well…*" She took a quick, nervous bite of her manicure. "I suppose I'm required by law to tell you the reason why the former residents of this beautiful home left in such a jiff."

"Whaa?" Mario stifled a frightened yelp. "What is it?"

"Oh, it's nothing, really. It's just a small detail." She found it hard to maintain eye contact with the writer. "Do you believe in the paranormal?"

"The paranormal," he repeated as his voice dropped an octave. "I guess. I write about it often enough. I've never experienced it, though. What exactly are you talking about?"

"Yaah… Well, you probably haven't anything to worry about. The former residents were rather superstitious, I suppose, but according to them, this trailer is haunted."

"Haunted." His tone was matter-of-fact and cautious. Possible, sure, but ridiculous.

Claren examined her nails. "Well, not just haunted, but possessed, like, by a demon. Have you ever heard of a succubus?"

Mario was well-versed in the occult and supernatural, as his works almost always dealt with the topic. Devils, demons, Djinn, the Goetia and all the rest of it would often populate his pages. As such, he had to research many of these beasties, but he wasn't ever certain that he believed in their actual existence.

"Yeah, the succubus is like some sort of sex demon, right?"

"Bingo!" Claren beamed. "Yaah… You allegedly have a succubus living in the attic."

"*What?*" Mario's eyes popped. "That's stupid."

"I know, right?" She made an attempt at empathy. "The former residents claimed her name is Lala and she's always, well, um... *horny?*"

Such nonsense was the last thing he needed in his life. Mario didn't even like to date; he thought it a waste of time and an interruption to his writing. Although most of his friends and contemporaries considered him to be a prude and frigid, the truth was that he simply preferred to focus his efforts and emotions on his craft. To think that his new home contained a resident sex monster filled his heart with a moment of intense dread.

"I can't be bothered with that," he all but pleaded. "I've got a lot of shit to do and a deadline to meet by the end of the month. How do we get rid of her?"

The agent shrugged her shoulders. "How should I know? Maybe call up an exorcist or something?"

"Yeah, but... "

"Look," she halted him. "Although she has a voracious appetite for sex, she's also very tidy. Think of her more like a live-in maid who likes to fuck a lot. You'll be fine. Just don't let her rinse you for your soul. She reportedly wakes up or manifests, or whatever you want to call it around 3 a.m."

"But I don't even like having sex at all," he protested. "What the fuck am I gonna do now?"

She split a quick smile and twirled her way toward the night's beckoning darkness. "You'll figure it out. I must be going, dear. I have one more deal to close before the evening is up. Have fun with your new home!"

"This is bullshit!" Mario volleyed as she walked at a brisk pace to her Audi. "So, what lives in *their* house, huh? Cthulhu?"

Claren didn't even bother to turn around as she flipped him the bird. He stood in the doorway, dumbstruck as a litany of horrible worries began to file past in his mind like a marching regiment of grotesque toy soldiers. It was at that point that Mario realized it had all been too good to be true and that he was, in fact, nothing less than a sucker.

* * *

Like a Gothic cliché, the towering grandfather clock in the living room ticked on and on. *Tick-tock, tick-tock*. It was now 7:15 p.m. He began rushing about the trailer, turning on every light he could find. In his novels, it always seemed that the featured victims were assaulted in the dark. He didn't want to make the same mistake and suffer their fate.

Illumination set his mind at ease, but only a little. Off to the right of the grand hall was a nondescript door. It was the door that Claren had failed to open during their tour. He knew damn well where it led — the attic.

Mario smacked himself on the forehead and cursed. When he had seen the beauty of the place on the Internet, he took the naïve route of arranging a deal without having an actual look at the property. "What the hell do I know about buying a house?" he whined to no-one.

Admittedly, the place was gorgeous. The hall's walls were portioned by elaborate moldings and Mario imagined just how wonderful the press-posters of his novels would look hanging in between them. All were designed with great craftsmanship by the renowned German artist Hauke Luger. He figured he would display them in order of release: *Liches Be Crazy, Smack*

My Lich Up and *The Seven Year Lich*.

Mario went to the games room. Playing an old-school video game might be just the thing to help soothe his nerves, he guessed. He chose to give *Dig-Dug* a shot; something goofy and challenging. After clearing a few levels, he gave the clock hanging on the wall behind him a cursory glance. It was 8:05 p.m. The journey to 3:00 a.m. was not going to be stopped. *Dreadful.*

As he watched in horror as the time passed, the tune of *Ding-Dong Merrily Along* rang throughout the house. *What the hell?* He winced. That had to be the mansion's doorbell.

"I hope it's that swindling Candace and that she left something behind," he grumbled aloud as he rushed to the front door. "I want to give that skank an earful."

He opened the door and found not the skank, but something that took a moment to register. Before him stood a man with Hollywood good looks wearing loud, purple overalls and a multicolored beanie hat complete with a whirligig. The man's oddest feature was that his smartly-trimmed beard was dyed bubblegum-pink, making him look like some kind of postmodernist clown. His hands held what appeared to be a covered cake plate.

"Sweet Jesus!" Mario hollered, clearly taken aback by the man's appearance. "Who the fuck are you?"

The freak before him gave a beaming, pink smile. His teeth were perfect. "It's cool, bro. I'm your neighbor, Kenny Loggins!"

Mario screwed his brows in confusion. "Oh, you're that guy who wrote the theme song to *Caddyschmuck* a million years ago,

160

right? My lousy real estate agent told me you lived next door."

"Guilty as charged, neighbor. Are you a fan?"

He shook his head. "Sorry, dude. I never really got into Golfpunk. No offense. By the way, what's up with the clown gear, Kenny Loggins?"

"Oh, this?" Kenny Loggins pointed to his beanie. "This isn't clown gear, bro. This is me being a brony."

Mario's wrinkled brow signaled his increasing confusion, and he leaned in, curious. "Eh...What's a brony?"

Kenny Loggins leaned back, shocked. "What? You've never heard of the bronies? Have you been living under a rock? We're like the coolest religion on earth. In a nutshell, we're rabid fans of *My Little Pony*; the new version, of course, not that shitty original one."

"Okay..." He still could not grasp what he'd just been told. "Not to be homophobic or anything, but that sounds kind of gay."

"No way!" Kenny Loggins returned. "Bronies hail from all kinds of orientations, even asexual. As a matter-of-fact, lots of bronies are big fans of your books."

"You don't say," Mario almost groaned.

Back when he began his writing career, Mario encountered many sorts of people in his budding fanbase. Some would praise, some would criticize, and a couple exhibited what could only be described as stalking behavior. He just couldn't grasp why someone would bother to pay attention to such an unassuming guy. Throughout college, it was a rarity if he even attended a small get-together, much less a kegger. In many ways, Mario felt invisible, and that suited him just fine, but as his work gained recognition, the fandom grew. It was much too alien and unnerving for him.

"Here," Kenny Loggins thrust forth the cake plate. "It's just a little housewarming gift. I baked it myself."

"Uh, thanks, man." Mario said as he accepted the dessert. "At least someone's done something nice for me today."

A look of genuine concern washed across the has-been's face. "What's the problem, bro? Moving-in blues? Shoot, that'll pass."

"More like I got banged up the ass by the real estate wench," said Mario. "This trailer is supposedly possessed by a demon from Hell or some such nonsense, and the bitch is going to try to rape me at three in the morning." Mario shook his head in embarrassment. "That's stupid. I can't believe I even said anything. How can I be so gullible?"

Kenny Loggins nodded. "Yeah, I heard something about that back when the Orphanblenders moved away. They lived here before you. Those dorks ran out of the place screaming their heads off in the middle of the night, hopped in their minivan and I never heard from them again. But they were total religious nuts. Probably just saw a shadow and thought it was the Devil or something."

"Sure, but maybe there's some merit in their claims?"

Smiling, Kenny Loggins rested his hand on Mario's shoulder. The gesture only helped to ramp up his nerves. He detested such unwarranted contact.

"Hey, bro. I've got an idea. Sounds like you could use some company. We should hold a housewarming party for you tonight, dude. I'll invite all my friends and we could be back over here in an hour. Hell, I'll even provide the entertainment. What do you say?"

Never before had he hosted a party. Going to one was bad enough, but the thought of having to entertain an old rock star's entourage was nothing less than a chilling prospect. Even more frightening was the possibility of whether or not they'd be a gaggle of "bronies."

Then again, Mario considered, there might be safety in numbers. If this succubus were to make an appearance at the party, perhaps she would be more inclined to accost one of Kenny Loggins's cohorts instead?

"Okay," Mario relented. "It's a deal."

"It's a deal, bro," Kenny Loggins flashed a thumbs-up. "I'll start making the calls. See you in an hour or so."

"By the way, my name's Mario."

"Yeah, I know."

* * *

The kitchen clock reported 8:40 p.m. Now, Mario had the grief of not only worrying about a sexual assault from beyond, he had a goddamned party to host too. *What an awful night*, he thought. He wondered if he could forfend the succubus's appearance by boarding the attic door up, but she most likely possessed supernatural strength and would just bash it apart.

Lifting the lid off the plate, he was greeted by yet another peculiarity. The design adorning the face of the cake was that of a confectionary cartoon depicting a purple unicorn pony ramming its horn into the Human Torch's flaming butthole. Thick blue frosting announced that "Neighbors are Magic!" The thing reeked of Fruity Pebbles.

"What the hell is this shit?" he questioned the lonely kitchen. He buried his face in his hands and moaned. "Hell, nothing makes any sense today."

As he turned to his left, Mario saw that horrid doorway almost pulsating, beckoning. Would it be wise to give it a shot, he wondered? After all, the worst that could happen would be the rousing of an infernal beast.

Screw it, he decided. He wanted to put an end to this mystery and find out that his anxiety was fueled by nothing but imagination. Mustering what small reserve of courage he had, Mario marched up to the door and, with a trembling hand, slowly turned the doorknob.

An unfinished staircase led to his goal: the attic. It was quite unlike the rest of the mobile home as it boasted none of the grace or design of any of the other rooms. This portion of the place seemed like an architectural afterthought.

Each step creaked and squeaked and he knew if she was indeed there, he'd lose any initiative. Initiative against what, he mused? There was no such thing as a succubus. Not really.

Luckily, the attic had juice in the lights. The small chamber was as well-lit as any other room in the mobile mansion. Three windows treated him to a rather impressive view of the surrounding neighborhood. The sky had finally cleared and starlight competed with the Tiffany chandelier's illumination. *Kind of nice.*

Nothing much to see, just as he suspected. A couple of old

164

trunks, a naked mannequin and a dusty full-length mirror occupied the space. Typical attic shit.

How ridiculous, he thought. There were no demons from Hell lurking in the few shadows the room had to offer.

"Ollie, Ollie Oxen-Free!" he belted to the emptiness. "Yoo-hoo! Lala! Where you at, girl?"

Half expecting to be set upon from places unknown, Mario braced himself for attack, but when no such assault was forthcoming, he realized that the only thing he would have to deal with was what his rationale had assumed all along—nothing.

One feature was of interest, however: upon the southern wall was what appeared to be a scorch mark in the design of a vague, hourglass-shaped human form. Mario scored his fingertips across it, but found nothing more than a dry, dark stain. He knocked on it three times and waited a spell. Again—nothing.

"Just what I thought," he said. "This is lame."

He ambled down the stairs, somewhat disappointed, before suddenly stopping in his tracks. "Shit!" he hissed. "Now I have to entertain a bunch of clowns for nothing. Kenny Loggins sucks."

Once again, he passed by the grandfather clock. Time still flew by. It was now 9:35 p.m. The nerds would be arriving at any moment.

Mario opened the pantries and the refrigerator, only to find every one of them cleared out. He still had to go to the store at some point, but it didn't matter if he was deemed a poor host because he didn't want to moderate a party anyway.

Looking down at his fingernails, he realized that he'd been biting them the entire evening. He made a mental note to either calm down or get some therapy for his anxiety issues. It wasn't every day that someone was warned they might be assailed by forces from the nether planes of existence, after all. "I really need to get a dog or something," he said to his desolate kitchen.

There was still an array of dishware, cutlery and other utensils left behind in the cupboards and cabinets. Mario decided to make good use of the time he had left by arranging them for the mob of morons who would soon be arriving, courtesy of a certain washed-up rock star. Here, he also made a mental note not to be such a pushover in the future.

Knives, forks, spoons and plates were all set out to his best arrangement, considering the timely circumstances. It was only a half-assed attempt, as he hoped that this dumb soiree would be a short one. He found no napkins, so the guests would have to do without. Placing a saucer on a bar adjacent to the dining room, he nearly dropped and shattered it as the house was suddenly filled by the resonance of a sudden, annoying tune:

Ding-Dong Merrily Along!

"Oh, crap…" Mario protested.

Not really knowing why he was hustling to greet them, he bounded down the hall and skidded into the front door. Perhaps it was to call a halt to his awful doorbell's jingle? Mario clamped his eyes shut tight like a vise, held his breath, counted to three and opened the door.

* * *

"Surprise, neighbor!" cheered the throng in unison. What stood before Mario was nothing but a garish cavalcade, an eyesore of epic proportions. Rainbow-colored shirts and skirts. Loud bowties of every color of the visible spectrum and buttons and badges boasting *My Little Pony* regalia glittered in the glow of the porch light. Their hairdos were worse. Not one of the myriad among them possessed a hue known by humankind to be natural. Lots of pinks and purples, but a couple of specimens had baby-blues and lime-greens.

Mario stood gobsmacked at this saccharine display. Aside from looking like people spun from sugar, there was something wrong with their faces. The eyes of each were glazed over in a permanent, holy reverence. To what, he could only guess, but it was apt to stand on four legs.

"Hey, bro," Kenny Loggins said. "Told you I'd be back. Got a lot o' sweet peeps here with me and a big surprise for you."

"Uh, c-cool," Mario stammered. "Come on in, I guess."

They filed in like they owned the place, and Mario supposed that was all right for now. Truth be told, he did invite them in an oblique way. The only question now was how to get rid of them? He'd think of something, sooner or later.

"Everybody!" Kenny Loggins announced. "This is my new neighbor, Mario Poon! He's the totally awesome dude who writes all those Lichpunk books. Let's give him a big, brony round of applause!"

"Neighbors are magic!" they chanted like brainwashed Satanists. "MLP forever!"

Oh, God, Mario cheeped in his mind as he tried to form a wan smile. *I should have taken a chance on the demon instead of this tripe.*

Kenny Loggins slung an arm around Mario's shoulder. He stiffened like a corpse from the unexpected shock of it.

"Man, I've got a lot of magical friends here for you to meet; fellow bronies and pegasisters from around the world. A few are celebrities just like me."

"Great to know," Mario mumbled. "By the way, where are your instruments? Didn't you say you'd provide the entertainment or something?"

"I sure did," Kenny Loggins said. "But it's not musical entertainment. It's *magical* entertainment."

The former rock star cupped his hands around his mouth and called, "Oh, Snap Apple! Come on in!"

Mario couldn't believe just what clip-clopped in through the front door. It held its head high and majestic, like it was the queen of the trailer. Not only was Mario aghast that a pony was plodding about in his new home, the fact that it was purple and had a spindly horn jutting from its forehead while one large, feathered wing protruded from its right flank induced an element of surrealism to the proceedings.

What the fuck?

"Eh, Kenny Loggins? I've heard of dog and pony shows, but is that a purple unicorn in my house?"

"It sure is, bro." Kenny Loggins shot out his hand like some sort of ringmaster. "Mr. Poon, please meet Snap Apple."

"Hi, S-Snap Apple," the writer managed. He still couldn't believe that he had just greeted a one-winged unicorn, and he strained his eyes to see if the horn was attached by strings or adhesives. To his surprise, he found neither. This thing appeared to be the real deal, but what happened next made poor Mario faint.

168

"Pleased to meet your acquaintance, I'm sure," the equine monstrosity responded with a haughty purr. "Kenny Loggins has told me all about you."

* * *

A sweet scent invaded his nostrils and smacked his brain alive. Kenny Loggins stood before Mario with the ridiculous cake hovering in front of his face. It took a moment to register why his wrists were aching, until he realized that he was bent over a sofa and that his hands were bound to the armrests.

"Help!" Mario shouted. "I'm all tied up."

"Hey, bro," Loggins attempted an assuring tone. "It's all for your own good. Snap Apple has to get her other wing somehow."

"So what the hell does that have to do with me being tied up, you twat lord?"

Loggins began to pace before the arrested writer. "You see, Mario Poon, in order for our dear Snap Apple to become an alicorn, she needs one final ingredient—your soul."

"What the fuck is an alicorn?" Mario hollered.

"Why, it's a unicorn with wings, bro. She certainly can't fly with just one."

The grimness of Mario's situation hit home in a sudden moment of clarity. That goofy graphic embellishing the cake wasn't merely a decoration; it was a grim hieroglyphic, a testament to what had once happened and a warning sign of what was in store for him.

"I get it, you bastard," the writer seethed. "That stupid

cartoon on the cake was Will Smith! Snap Apple rammed her horn up his ass!"

Kenny Loggins folded his arms and gave an arrogant grin. "You got it, bro, and she's about to do the same to you. After all, how else can she acquire souls? She just sucks them right out through your lowest chakra. As for poor Will, we had to burn the body afterwards and cover it up with a tale of a terrible accident. But enough with the gloating. It's time to cut them britches loose."

Two fellow bronies yanked said britches to the floor. Mario could feel his rarely used balls shrivel from a combination of the chill of the ambient temperature and mortal fear. From somewhere behind, he could hear Snap Apple grunting and brushing a hoof against the tile like a bull preparing to charge a matador. Mario Poon gritted his teeth and commenced kissing, literally, his ass goodbye.

Through the din of the heinous party a loud bang echoed from down the hall that had the immediate effect of silencing the revelers. The sound of high heels clacking against the tile resounded with metered confidence and poise. A feminine yawn sailed through the living room-cum-luau. Brony and pegasister alike gasped in unison.

"And what have we here?" asked this latest arrival. "It looks like a solid orgy complete with a pony and *I* wasn't invited?"

A pegasister from somewhere off to Mario's right shrieked, "Who the hell are you?"

"Excellent question," the new arrival cooed. "Lala Atibon is who the *hell* I am."

"It's the succubus!" Kenny Loggins stabbed a finger at the

demoness. "She *is* real!"

"Of course I am," Lala said. "And I need to know only one thing: just who is the new lord of this mobile manor?"

Mario mustered the nerve to open his eyes. Lala stood before him at a height well over six feet. As far as Mario was concerned, a woman was never much more than a neutral stimulus, but this goddess before him was a different story: blood-red hair as straight as a poker with the bluntest of bangs cascaded mere inches above the floor. Her bitch boots were hewn of hellish black leather and boasted heels eight inches high. She wore not much more. There was something vulpine about her face—and it was nothing less than beautiful. For a moment, Mario feared popping an erection, but then he remembered that his pants were around his ankles.

Embarrassed to admit it in front of this gorgeous hellion, considering his circumstances, the doomed writer lifted a bound hand as far as was possible. "Erm... that would be me."

"Ah, the host is also the guest of honor. And what might your name be, mortal?"

"Mario Poon," he squeaked.

"Poon..." Lala savored his surname on her forked tongue. "A fine word, one that I am well acquainted with."

Mario craned his neck and glanced at a nearby clock. "I thought you weren't supposed to wake up until 3 a.m. or such."

She huffed at that, flipped her hair. "Well, if someone hadn't awoken me by knocking on my portal, I would still be asleep. Alas, I am roused and here we all are. This soiree of yours did not help matters, by any means. Nevertheless, I am here to liberate you from this tawdry frying pan so that I may take you to my proverbial fire, yes?"

A grunt and a whinny interrupted the demon's lecture. Snap Apple was not pleased with the new attention Mario had secured. "Who does this bitch think she is? Poon's ass is mine!"

"Oh, really, little horsie?" Lala challenged. "And what makes you assume that you may lay claim to such a fine posterior, hmm?"

"Mario Poon is the author of the *Lichpunk Trilogy*," the four-legged freak of nature began. "Whether he likes it or not, his volumes are a testament to Brony culture. More to the point, *I need his fuckin' soul!*"

Lala liked this not one bit. As a growl brewed in her innards, her red irises began to animate, morphing into inverted pentagrams. Snap Apple met the demon's simmering rage and commenced stamping a hoof against the tile, prepared to pounce. *Clop, clop, clop.*

The succubus produced a wicked, barbed whip from underneath her scant French maid's outfit and sliced the air with it. Its resulting crack was quite hellish. "And Mario needs to get laid!" As such, the massacre of 1127 Hairball Drive began.

Two preternatural beasts careened into each other through the stuffy air of that spacious living room. The twain locked onto each other in a death clutch. Lala's whip swirled hither and yon without care while Snap Apple donkey-kicked with just as little concern.

Jeff Lynne caught two hooves in his periwinkle beard, thus imploding his head. Kim Carnes was decapitated by a wild swing of Lala's whip. Some dude who looked like Freddie Mercury, but who wasn't Freddy Mercury was kicked into the large (and very expensive) plasma screen television and was duly electrocuted. Blood, entrails, limbs and the worst fashion violations ever known to man sprayed the walls of that posh mobile home as a result of the fracas.

Kenny Loggins ducked, bobbed and jumped, but to no avail. The succubus's whip sliced both of his feet from his ankles and he fell to the floor like a gunnysack. His blood loss was so great that his Hollywood tan blanched away in seconds.

With a weave and a feint, Lala caught Snap Apple's horn with her hellish weapon. It noodled up and down the thing in a spiral. There was only one way for the unicorn to break free.

Snap Apple's horn flew into the demon's hand. Deep blue gore dripped from its stump, only adding to the mess.

Defeated, the unicorn slumped to the ground, screeching from the pain in her head. Lala caught her boot's heel around the beast's neck.

"As you can see, dear Snap Apple," Lala boasted. "*I'm* the only horny one here!"

"NO!" cried Snap Apple, but it was too late. Her heartwrenching pleas were cut short as the succubus skewered her with her own weapon right through her equine head.

The living room looked worse than that of a shithouse in the battle's aftermath. There would be no way to return it to normal, Mario feared as he remained bound.

Lala sauntered over to him, love-tapped his bare ass and said, "Good riddance to bad trash, yeah?"

"Yeah, I didn't know I had so many freakish fans." He looked up at her, eyes pleading. "Hey can you get me untied?"

She bent down to his subdued level, cocked a fine brow and gave him a crooked, lascivious smile. "Now, that all depends on whether or not you tie *me* up..."

* * *

Thigh Gap

The new fragrance by Miley Ray Cyrus.

Thigh Gap

From Coeur d'Alene and Crimpton.

Available at Bojingles.

The sex wasn't so bad, thought Mario as he dragged on his post-coital cigarette while the television sang forth banal commercials in his billowing west-wing bedroom. He was by no means a virgin, but romance and affection and all the other stuff that went along with it just weren't his cup of tea.

Sure, he found some women attractive, but in his few relationships, he only proved to make them miserable and feeling somewhat ignored. Such a dynamic confused him at first, only to make him feel bad for them later on in life. He was far too consumed by his fantasies of dragons, cool fucking robots, liches and heroes and heroines to pay them the proper amount of attention. Perhaps this was a personality defect, but it ended up paying off in some ways.

"Oh, hail Satan!" Lala pointed to the screen across the room. "That looks great! I, like, totally want a bottle of Thigh Gap. I just adore Miley Cyrus. That skank is *amazing!*"

Dear God, he groaned to himself. *They have valley girls in Hell.*

174

"Say, Lala. Where do you live, exactly?" he asked.

"I live in Salacia Heights on the outer ring of Avernus," she said, half listening while changing channels. "It's in the first layer of Hell. It's okay, I guess. My apartment's like, pretty cool. My roommate, Hoggatha is a fucking bitch, though. I mean, the girl needs to wash her ass or I'm just going to shoot myself in the face."

Lala turned over and lent him a sincere smile. "You know, Mario. Nobody up here is nice to me, like you are. Most people just call up those stupid exorcists and stuff on me when they move in. They don't talk to me about important things like you do. Well, except for those stupid Goth kids, but they just want to ask me if Hell is full of dead heavy metal stars and stupid junk like that."

His eyes widened. *Not this shit again…*

"Hey, Lala. All this sex and stuff has made me really hungry. There's an In-Out/In-Out Burger over on Baculum Boulevard and it's open all night. What do you say we hop into the car and get one?"

Her eyes brightened to that suggestion. "Hell, yeah! I could eat a horse! Pun not intended, but yeah, let's go."

Mario rolled over to her. "Speaking of which, you destroyed a lot of bronies down there. My living room is totally trashed."

She waved it off. "No worries. I'll clean it up tomorrow night. I can just burn all the bodies of those morons in the crematorium down in your backyard."

Mario shot up to this news. "I have a crematorium in my backyard?"

"For sure," she nodded, still watching TV. "This place used to be a mobile funeral home back in the '70's. Lots of Disco-fueled coke overdoses back then. Dude, those were the days. Rick Ocasek was cremated here. Pretty cool, huh?"

"Yeah, I guess," Mario shrugged. "Let's get out of here."

The night was a whirlwind of fine, tepid air and the coastal highway was a treat of heavenly moonlight. Mario's Subaru Celexa purred along with the chirp of horny crickets. He had not experienced such a night of joy since he'd driven home from his first book signing.

As for Lala, she was growing on him. Neither of the pair were the gushy types, and that suited him just fine. Although she was far from human, she wasn't the worst of mates, he supposed as he recollected the times spent with his litany of exes. Besides, he loved how her crimson locks flew about in the slipstream of the breeze.

Without a word, she punched the car's sound system and the blast of REO Speedwagon's *Roll With the Changes* destroyed the fine ambience. Mario winced from sonic shock.

"Ew!" he protested. "Gotta change this." He re-tuned to the indie station KNOX and settled on that.

The plaintive strains of Daniel Johnston's *True Love Will Find You in the End* flooded the vehicle. Mario always thought of him as an obsession for the pretentious, but as he looked over at Lala's happy face, he found that the song kind of fit the mood.

True or not, this might be love. Sometimes one must choose the lesser of two evils. As with all of his past relationships, there was no guarantee, but Mario decided that in the end, he'd prefer to enjoy love, even if only for a short time, rather than have a purple unicorn's horn jammed up his ass.

Even in Hell.

'Sniffing the Air'

by Val Tenterhosen

I were out washing socks in the crick when they caught the sunna bitch. Real low down dirty son of a fucker, too, dripping with horseflesh and rearing to kill him some more of us ignorant river folk. I could hear him hollering from a ways off. I left the damn socks and got my shit together quick.

I had been around the block a time or two and I knew this mother's bastard child would be one unruly cousinfucker of a shit. I went down with a sawed-on and decided to cook me up some cornbread.

"Time for a little snack," I says when I sees him.

He was standing there in chains, a few of the townsfolk all around him. My oldest littun put a hand on my chest.

"No, paw," said little Betty. "He's only fourteen years old. He's got his whole life a'fore him."

"Stow it, Betts. I'm going to boil this varmint in oil for what he thinks he did to Ms. Hightower. Crabtree can come down here himself if he wants to stop me."

"Be a waste o' oil," the dickslapper said to me, chewing his cud calmer than a litter of shit.

"You keep out of it, pigeonplugger!" I cried.

"You want me to keep out of you killin' me? Fine," he said as placid as you please. "Let me the fuck out of here and I'll stay out of it all together."

Betty actually laughed at that, that stone-eyed son of bitch's whore, so I whacked her with the sawed-on. I twernt thinking, just reacting to that slut's mother of a smile on her face.

"See," says cockmuncher McGillicuddy, all knowing-like. "Yore as bad as the rest of 'em. Yore as bad as me."

"Fuck 'em!" I said, and I took the sawed-on and took out every bitchbooger in the place save for that shitweaseling little fartfucker. I took out the last four shells and put them in my pocket. I walked up as close to that broadbrained frog-for-shit dickslinger as I dared and slammed the sawed-on into his grimy little booger hands.

"You're a fuckin' turd, you know that, bitchweasle?"

I turned around and started hollerin' all half-assed for help.

"Help, help! They've been shot!" and all such sorts of shit.

They came and arrested old dickface just as much as they already woulda, and the dipshit hung for his crimes. But the good news is, all those other fuckers were dead, too.

I went back to cleaning my socks, and after a while, I started hoping for something else to happen. I sorta started strainin' my ears.

180

'Mr. Snake Eyes'

by Troy Blackford

1

The other day, I awoke to the sound of the bathroom mirror exploding.

I walked calmly down the hall, stepped gingerly over shards of glass, and found a single dead rat sticking out of one of the pieces. Not impaled upon one of the dagger-like fragments, but literally embedded in it, as though the rodent had been swimming through the mirror when it exploded.

I picked the shard up and looked at it. I lost track of time. When I finally set it back down, it was already dark out. I coughed, and when I pulled my hand away from my mouth, the word 'BANG!' was written in gold ink on my palm. I vomited on the shards of glass that still littered my bathroom floor.

I drank a glass of water and went back to bed. I couldn't sleep. I kept rubbing my hand where the gold lettering appeared, and it eventually started to flake off my skin.

I must have fallen asleep at some point, because the next thing I knew, I was running through trees that lined a kind of makeshift trail. When I peered through the foliage to orient myself, I could descry a sprawling golf course, obscured by the leaves. I ran out of the woods and found myself near a lobby. I walked inside.

A man in a three-piece suit with a kind of frog's head looked up at me in surprise when I entered. He was playing a pinball machine, and when I walked in he seemed surprised to see me.

"Weatherby!" he cried, as though I were someone he hadn't seen in years. "What brings you to the Farmridge Branch of Sunny Acres?"

"Dirt trail," I said, truthfully.

He nodded as though this was explanation enough, and his focus returned to his pinball game. I walked over and looked at the cabinet he was playing. The glowing marquee read "*Exprime Complémentaire.*"

A loud gong sounded and I walked outside. A train track started at the door and led away from the lodge, across the golf course. I decided to follow.

The track went perfectly straight for nine miles before curving at an overlook set high above the ocean. I took in this view for some time, lost in the reflections of sunlight coming off the blue waves, before I heard a loud whistle. The train was coming.

I stepped to the side and watched passively as a nine-hundred-and-sixty-two car train hurtled by at immense speed. After an hour, the caboose finally rolled by. I continued my journey.

"Don't forget about the lockets, child."

I turned around to see where the voice had come from. It hadn't come from anywhere. I hadn't heard it, I reasoned. I walked on.

The lockets didn't exist so how could I forget about them?

182

I reached a spot that seemed as good a place as any to rest so I began to dig into the earth with a small spade that had been left there for precisely that purpose. One, two, three strikes with the spade and soon I was underground.

In the underground corridor below, I noticed row after row of LED rope lighting hanging from the earthen ceiling. Using this for navigation, I walked ten steps north, four steps east, looped around and continued to walk for sixteen hundred and forty two steps. I stopped.

Using a pole provided for just such an occasion, I prodded at the dirt above me until I had poked a suitable hole in the roof of the underground tunnel. Not exactly knowing where I was, I nevertheless felt comfortable taking a flying leap upwards and clawing my way out of the hole. Seventeen and a half seconds later, I had succeeded.

Once more on the surface of the earth, I saw nothing but glittering stars all around me. I took four steps and touched the closest with my wand. It shivered, but continued to give off light. Removing my shoes and placing them in a sack, I ducked twice and curled up upon the cold but brightly glowing star. I then fell asleep.

It was at this point that I awoke to a loud shrieking sound.

I went to my bathroom, and saw a head emerging from the depression at the bottom of the toilet. It was screaming. I picked up one of the sharp fragments of glass still on my bathroom floor, and dipped my hand into the toilet water. The head continued to squeal as I dug the tip of the mirror shard into the neck and, using a sawing motion, removed the head.

I placed the head in the bathtub. I proceeded to wash my hands and brush my teeth and then went to my refrigerator.

Inside, I found a box of Arm and Hammer baking soda intended to keep the fridge smelling nice and fresh. I reached into my cabinet, grabbed a clean glass, poured the baking soda inside, and added water. Stirring with a steak knife, I drank the mix in two big gulps.

I spat up a little but otherwise there were no effects.

I turned on the television and saw a commercial, followed by another commercial. A show came on, so I swiftly turned channels until I found another commercial. Two commercials later, I had had my fill of TV so I went on a bathroom break.

I was beginning to feel sleepy around this time, so I bent over and vomited onto the carpet. It seemed to fizz, likely on account of the baking soda. I moved on, opening my broom closet and crawling inside.

I hid in the closet for four hours and twenty two minutes until I came out and went to sleep.

I woke up back in the dream, still on my star and once again next to a train. I used a can of gas and a lighter to fill the lighter, then I replaced the lighter and gas can where I had found them. Going to the woods, I picked up two sticks and began to vigorously rub them together until I produced a spark.

Two gas cans later, I had enough lighters to fill the train. This task complete, I moved on to woodworking. I had enough wood to work with, so I carved them into sixteen swans, ninety fish, and two fish. I then set fire to them all with a gas can.

Time had come. I moved on. Two days later, I came to a carving of a finch. Using a pocketknife, I whittled this into a fish and then into a swan. Scooping up the wood shavings, I added them carefully to a glass of water and then drank that glass. It turned into a murky solid which I then expelled at a rate of sixteen CCs per incidence.

I was beginning to grow sleepy again so I took off my shoes once more. This was the start of something monumental so I also deigned to remove my socks, which I placed inside the shoes for safe keeping. Thus exposed to the elements, I created a pile of wood fourteen inches high and crawled upon it to sleep.

I woke up at my farm. I trotted over to the pigs and carved one into a swan and took the shavings, cooked them, and ate the resulting bacon for forty-five minutes. I then shaved and added the cuttings to a pile marked 'To Be Saved Later.'

Four more minutes was all I had, so I had to do something quick. Finding a spark and a sharpshooter's mask, I took off both fish and added myself to the following lists: 'Cod,' 'Door,' 'Fin.'

I found the frog man again but he didn't call me Weatherby. I added him to the list 'Tin,' 'Rope,' and 'Annulment.' Walking to the store, I bought two leashes and tied them both to the dog labeled 'Indices.' He remarked that it would make more sense for his name to be 'Index,' so we marched promptly to the courthouse where I had my name legally changed to 'Indice.'

We had two swan carvings left at this point, so I set a fire and crawled into a van left along the side of the road. It was filled with two old men and a bag of candy. They prodded me with instruments and deposited me in a sort of upside-down river that took me forty-five seconds and two minutes to make my way out of.

I coughed out two liters of upside-down river water and decided to go shopping for fishheads at the local market.

Leaving my dog behind, I snatched up a broomstick and two watersheds and took the measure of every fishhead in the store. One, two, three dithyrams and a whacking sort of forehead noise later, I had the information I needed so I decided to pour myself a glass of orange rinds and call it a night.

The people around me vociferously objected, insisting that I should call it, rather, a 'glass of orange rinds.' I found this rigidity distasteful, and was about to tell them so, when I fell promptly asleep. I awoke inside a dream within a dream, a large label sticking out of my forehead.

It read, simply "Doormat."

It was then that I realized the true state of my predicament.

2

The frog of it was, I already knew it. I had fallen into the wrong hands. I simply hadn't done anything to rectify it. By piling goosepimple onto goosepimple, I had buried myself into a corner without eating it, too. A note struck my desk and when I read it I realized that I thought I began to begin to understand.

"This is a summons," read the note. "Please come immediately."

I brushed the goosepimples aside and climbed out of the gorge. I walked down the hallway and sat in front of the desk of one Mr. Anthony T. Pike. He nodded curtly.

"I see you received my summons," he said by means of an introduction. "There seems to have been an accident at the fire store."

186

"When was this?"

"Sunday, last," he said, folding his hands and placing them on the desk.

"That would certainly explain a lot of things."

"Well, that's the thing," he said, becoming tentative. "It would and it wouldn't."

"How's that?"

"There have been certain... events, Mr. Pammelstock. Certain events which cannot be undone."

"Most events can't," I responded, ignoring the fact that Mr. Pammelstock isn't my name.

"We have to..." Pike trailed off, looked down at his hands. "We have to unplug you in the next couple days, Mr. Pammelstock."

"And I have to unplug you, you ungrateful son of a bitch."

He nodded slowly. He seemed to expect this. He looked back up from his hands.

"May I ask you a question?"

"You just did," I replied.

"May I ask you a second question?"

"You just did."

"Can I at least ask it first?"

"Which question?"

"The one I want to ask?"

"Is it worse than all these other questions?"

"Much," he replied.

"I like the way you got out of that."

"Is that a tacit demonstration of permission?"

"That can't be your question."

"I'm going to be blunt."

"Go for it."

"I wasn't asking for permission."

I smiled at him.

"Why not?"

"Because," Pike said, leaning back in his chair and smiling back. "I am taking your response to the summons as a tacit demonstration of permission for me to make certain statements and ask certain questions."

"Of me?"

"That's right."

"But, in a deeper sense, I'm asking: of *me*, personally?"

"In this instance, yes."

"But in other instances?"

"It would depend, in that case, on the identity of the person being summoned."

"But not," I mused aloud, "on their response to the summons? In that instance, I mean?"

"Oh, in every instance, the entire proceedings inevitably depend on their response to the summons. So that's sort of taken as a given. In terms of influencing the rest of the proposition."

"But not as a response to the proposition itself?"

"No," Pike said, shaking his head. "Because in that case, we wouldn't need to wait for the response in order to determine if tacit demonstration of permission had been offered."

"Ahh, so the assumption of the acceptance of the response —"

" — would be interpreted as the assumptive determination of tacit permission, exactly." Pike nodded vigorously, as though he were pleased I was able to follow him to this logical point. "And that would invalidate the entire procedure."

"So," I said, becoming thoughtful, "this is procedure?"

He ignore this.

"May I ask the question?"

"You haven't done that yet?" I asked.

"Please, no questions," Pike said, placing both palms flat on the desk. "This is strictly off-the-record."

"So," I mused, "if I give you permission to ask this question, my answer will be off-the-record. That certainly changes things."

"No," Pike said, shaking his head. "Your answer would be a matter of public record. Only my answers to your questions — which, by the way, you do not have permission to ask — are to be kept off the books."

"So, I'm being recorded."

"Not in so many words, no."

I leaned back in the chair.

"I think you've earned the right," I said at last, "to ask a few questions."

"What made you decide that?"

"You've obviously gone to great lengths and put a great deal of thought into all of this. You have two more."

Pike nodded.

"Only one more will do, Mr. Pammelstock. Where were you on the night you were at home, cutting that head out of your toilet with the shards of mirror?"

"I know the night you mean," I said, steepling my fingers and resting my chin on them. "On the night in question, I was in Tuesday."

"I suspected as much. We saw the missing star and slept on it."

"Actually, I was the one sleeping on it."

"On what?"

"On a star. And that is your final question."

"I suspected as much. And when we awoke the next day, after ruminating about that piece of evidence, it all clicked into place."

"I'm very glad to hear it."

"So am I."

We sat there in silence for what seemed like a protracted moment.

"Anything else?" I asked at last, when the silence had become unbearable.

"Please," Pike said, shaking his head. "No questions."

"I never agreed to that."

"You did demonstrate," he said, rising quickly to his feet, "tacit permission when you responded to the summons."

"How do I know that?"

"You are being deliberately difficult. I shall have to call the guard."

"What guard?"

"*Please stop*," he said, cringing.

I could see that my line of questioning was causing him pain.

"What's in the syringe?"

"I asked you very nicely to stop," he said, and plunged the needle deep into my neck.

I never found out what was in the syringe, but I did pass out and when I woke up fourteen and three-fifths hours later I was naked, covered in Vaseline, and feeling very thirsty.

3

I was also back in my house. I strained my eyes listening for the screaming from the head in the toilet, but I heard nothing. Then I remembered: I had killed whoever that was with my mirror. The guilt was asphyxiating. I had never killed a human before.

I went into my gun closet and took out the highest-powered sniper rifle I could find. If I was going to be a murderer, I was at least going to do it right. I checked the chambers and saw everything was in order. I started looking for my sunglasses. Now that the slaughter bug had bit me, I was ready to get out there and do this. Then I heard a weird sound from the bathroom. I was getting pretty used to that by now.

I placed my palms on the hallway wall and hoisted myself up to the ceiling. Hand over hand, I swung towards the bathroom door like I was moving along monkey bars. Soon, I had made it. I dropped down onto both feet. I thought I really stuck the landing. A panel of judges held up cards in sequence: 10.0, 10.0, 10.0, Snake Eyes.

That last judge can really get you.

Putting thoughts of my bruised pride to one side for a moment, I turned back to the matter at hand. It had a mass of sixteen micrograms and the faint odor of salt. I didn't know what it was. I turned away from the matter and turned back to the strange noise in the bathroom that had brought me here.

I peeked in and saw nothing. Too dark. I turned on the light and then turned down its advances. It called me a blueballer. I then unscrewed the bulb, which it found to be overkill. I replaced it with a less lascivious bulb and activated the circuitry. The bulb proceeded to glow at a predetermined luminosity, revealing the source of the sound.

The mirror had reformed. That sound I heard was the noise the mirror shards made when they fused back together. The rat was still embedded in one of the shards. He was wriggling, and obviously stuck.

"I'm a *she*!" the rat cried in dismay. "Although all the parts that make that obvious are stuck in the mirror."

"Fair enough," I said, not as concerned with the rat's gender as the rat itself seemed to be.

"Oh, so you know I'm a girl, and you still think of me as 'it?'"

I shrugged.

"You're a rat," I answered.

The rat sighed, shook her head for a moment, and then continued to wiggle. Nothing doing. Still stuck in the cat. I mean mirror.

"God, I'm glad it's not a cat. At least I have a chance of getting out of a mirror."

"Is there something you want to talk about, rat?"

I was eager to get back to looking for my sunglasses. I was ready to go on a killing spree.

"Yeah, there's a lot to talk about, unfortunately. You're

losing it. And they're so close. It's like part of you knows that they are going to unplug you soon. You don't know whether to fight or give up. I think most of you has given up, and the rest of you is fighting. The fighting part is stronger."

"Yeah, well..." I said, uncertain how to go on with this conversation. "Do you have anything to say compelling enough to stop me from this murderous rampage? Because it's sounding more and more fun the longer I talk to you."

"Listen! Michael! I'm trying to tell you: this is your last chance. They're going to unplug you in twenty-four hours. If you can hear me, and can wake up, you have to do it now. There *is* no later."

"Then I better find my sunglasses ASAP," I responded curtly. "Now, if that's all you wanted to talk about, I better get going."

"I would like nothing more," the rat said.

"Well," I said, spinning the assault rifle around and gripping it by the barrel like a baseball bat, "I like you *less*, Mr. Wasp."

Then I really went at it. With the rifle, I mean. The mirror burst into almost as many bits as it had been in when it first exploded. Good times. The irritating wasp rat was all sort of stuck out of the shard still, like before. But it wasn't moving any more, and it certainly wasn't talking. I was pleased.

What could it have possibly been talking about? *Unplugging.* I felt like I had heard that somewhere before. I didn't buy it for a second. It was all just a load of fishguts.

What I was going to do was climb the highest building in town and then rain down sparks from my semi-automatic or whatever type of rifle I had. I looked on the stock.

194

"EXPLODING HEAD SHOOTER GUN" was embossed on the metal just above the trigger.

"It is altogether fitting and proper that we do this," I said, checking my six fanny packs for huge amounts of weaponbullets. All in place, just as they should be.

"It doesn't need to be like this, Michael," said a voice in the mirky darkness of the bathroom. I chatted up the lightbulb until it was once more turned on.

"Dammit, Mr. Wasprat! I am so sick of your confounded fetters!"

"Not I, not I," said the dead rat, silently.

This was bullshit. I needed a dead rat talking to me like I needed a hole in my head. I percussively flattened the dead rat wasp with the back of my gun. It was gunky. And I hadn't thought about it too good in advance because I would need to take my gun around to do the shootkilling and now it was all ratgut gunky. Dick move on my part.

"Michael, you can still do it," came that same voice.

"How speak you, flat rat?" I asked, all askance at the panic I was starting to feel. But that wasn't the answer. I realized that the rat wasn't the one talking.

I looked into the bathtub. The severed head I had deposited in there earlier was looking up at me with its glassy eyeballs.

"What kind of pronoun do you get?" I asked. I went to scratch my head and then worried it would be rude, considering the circumstances.

"Michael, you have to wake up."

"Me too!" I said, trying to laugh it off. "Besides," I added, my voice becoming sly, "my name is Indice."

"Please, Michael."

The head was kind of stuck in the same topical rut as the rat had been.

So I did what any self-respecting man about to go on a murder rampage would do when a severed head in his bathtub kept telling him to wake up: I took aim with my high-powered weaponrifle and indicated 'explode' with my index finger. That put an end to the talk in my bathroom.

It also spread a thin but putrid layer of pulped up rat guts from the weapon onto my finger. I wasn't happy. I didn't like rat guts. Luckily, I was in the bathroom so I was able to give my hands a quick wash before I went about my business.

"Time to get to the busyparts," I said gleefully as I finished up wiping off the rifle. No more guts here.

I walked down the hallway and the whole building shook. Business shelves and rock hard paint images fell off the walls and exploded in a shower of sparks and ice cubes.

"Oh, marble wallets!" I cried as I steadied myself. What was this?

The ceiling split open like a milk carton and the air began to pour out. I coughed twice and then spun around, where I coughed six times. Breathing was hard.

This wasn't how it was supposed to be. What did that make me think of? I couldn't remember.

I remembered what everybody had said. About waking up.

Then I suddenly thought of Pascal's Wager. At least, I think that's what it was called. Anyway, the idea is that if you believe in something that happens after you die, and it's not true, oh well. Big whoop. But if you believe and it turns out true, you're better off. And everybody besides the rat and the frogman who called me Weatherby had been trying to say the same thing.

So I figured what the hell. It was a pretty easy thing to figure since all the air was pouring out of the house through a rip in the ceiling. There weren't, in fact, too many other things to think.

"I hereby resolve," I said, dropping the rifle, putting one hand behind my back, and holding the other one up like a boy scout taking the oath, "to sleep no more. It's wakefulness for me."

For a moment, the sparks and ice cubes kept piling up as more and more things exploded, but an instant later they all liquefied and started to flow out of the giant hole in the ceiling. I couldn't breathe in at all. With the last of my last breath, I cried out: "I'm awake! I'm awake!"

Everything drained away in an explosive moment, like a clap of thunder. My eyes winced painfully shut. I sat like that for what seemed like a long time. Except, I realized, I wasn't really sitting. I was lying down.

My lungs screamed for air, and yet it took longer than you would expect for me to even try to breathe. When I did, I was more than pleasantly surprised to find that it worked. The instant relief to my screaming lungs was heavenly. The breath itself felt rattly, like leafing through the brittle pages of an old, dusty book. But it worked. It worked great.

I was unable to see anything in the darkness, but shortly after

I got my lungs going again, I decided that there might be a chance that this was only because my eyes were closed. I tested this hypothesis and was pleased to find it was correct.

I couldn't tell what I was looking at, not at first. Everything was too bright. It seemed like a bright white light with a lot of dark little squiggles squirming around in it. I had to wonder what that meant. A second later I heard a sound I was not prepared for.

"*Beep.*"

The first thing I thought of was Sputnik. If I recall correctly, '*beep*' was about the only thing it could say. Dear lord, what if I were stuck in Sputnik?

That didn't make any sense. Sputnik probably wasn't this bright. I blinked a few times to acclimate my eyes, and I was — for the first time in long memory — shocked at what I saw.

"Rebecca?"

She was crying. She said she hadn't expected in a million years for me to actually do it, to wake up. Not only was she crying, but she looked about five years of pain, worry, and loneliness older than I remembered her. But, I saw with a jolt of mingled joy and regret, wearing her ring.

A doctor I didn't recognize stood there, holding a clipboard and looking shocked.

"Mr. Pemburton!" he said.

"You wouldn't happen to be Dr. Anthony T. Pike, by any chance?"

"That's right," he said, looking even more surprised. "So you could actually tell what was going on while you were in the coma?"

I shook my head, smiled at Rebecca, and squeezed her hand.

"A few bits and pieces got through," I said. I remembered the voice telling me to wake up. "The important parts."

Rebecca smiled at me.

I thought back to the froghead man, the talking rat, the underground cavern.

"But tell what was going on?" I smiled. "I certainly hope not."

"Thank god," said Dr. Pike, "because otherwise we weren't going to give you your rifle back, Pammelstock."

Rebecca smiled, and a wasp flew out of her mouth, hit the wall, and melted into the white surface. Soon the stinger morphed into the kicking hind legs of a white rat.

"Just kidding," the doctor said. Things quickly reverted to the way they had been a moment before. "You're fine."

The exploded head in the bathroom screamed. The stars winked out. Trains ran backwards.

"D'oh!" I said. "You had me there for a minute."

I pulled out my rifle and went to work.

Some people, with their jokes.

Biographies

Mercedes Yardley –

MERCEDES M. YARDLEY is a dark fantasist who wears stilettos and red lipstick. She is the author of the short story collection *Beautiful Sorrows,* the novella *Apocalyptic Montessa and Nuclear Lulu: A Tale of Atomic Love,* and THE BONE ANGEL trilogy. Her website is www.mercedesyardley.com.

Val Tenterhosen –

VAL TENTERHOSEN spent two years underground after the Y2K transition in case society collapsed. When he emerged, he found that it basically had anyway. He also came out of his backyard shelter with two unprintable novels and a shitload of bills. He now lives in the forests of Northern California, building furniture and nailing stories together.

Anthony Rapino –

ANTHONY J. RAPINO resides in Northeastern Pennsylvania, somewhere between the concrete of the city and the trees of the forest. On occasion, you'll find him moderating the feverish battles between the creatures of these two arenas. Whose side he's on is anyone's guess.

His debut novel, *Soundtrack to the End of the World,* is currently available, as is his short story collection, *Welcome to Moon Hill* and his newest release, "Loosely Enforced

Rules." When in doubt, his newest fiction can always be found carved inside a variety of autumn gourds.

For proof of his psychosis, visit his website: www.AnthonyJRapino.com

M.C. O'Neill –

M.C. O'NEILL is arguably sane, but the State has never put him where he belongs—an asylum.

Alternating between touching YA tales of solipsistic fantasy and Bizarro-fueled filth, O'Neill has little instinct for business. This is not a problem.

It's quite possible that his cheese is sliding off his cracker, but he cares for this not.

As the co-editor for Fireside Press, M.C. works like a chimp to provide fine anthologies which delve into the odd and absurd for other writers who don't have a home.

Todd Keisling –

TODD KEISLING is a writer of horror and speculative fiction, the author of the novels *A Life Transparent* and *The Liminal Man* (an Indie Book Award finalist), and the bestselling Kindle series *Ugly Little Things*. Born in Kentucky, he now lives with his wife and son somewhere near Reading, Pennsylvania. He still has a day job, he's awkward and weird, and if you were to live next door to him your grass would probably die. Connect with him at his website, www.toddkeisling.com.

David Eccles –

DAVID ECCLES writes the tales that prevent him from sleeping night after night. He feels they have a life of their own and deserve a full and long life, which is why he releases them onto the page. His stories are often tinged with sadness and a typically British sense of humor. His first collection of flash fiction and short stories, Darke Times and Other Stories, is well reviewed and available in all popular e-book formats. He has previously been featured on various blogs and websites, including BOOKSoftheDEADPRESS.com. His work can be read in six of James Ward Kirk's anthologies, *Sex, Drugs & Horror, Serial Killers Tres Tria, Bones, Ugly Babies, Cellar Door 2,* and *Memento Mori.*

Tom Bordonaro –

TOM BORDONARO is a digitally reclusive author with contributions appearing in SHOCK TOTEM and a wild sense of humor.

John Boden –

JOHN BODEN lives a stone's throw from Three Mile Island with his wonderful wife and sons. A baker by day, he spends his off time writing and working on Shock Totem. He likes Diet Pepsi, heavy metal and sports ferocious sideburns. While his output as a writer is fairly small, it has a bit of a reputation for being unique. His work has appeared in 52 STITCHES, METAZEN, BLACK INK HORROR, WEIRDYEAR, NECON E-BOOKS, SHOCK TOTEM, the John Skipp edited PSYCHOS, SPLATTERPUNK and his "children's book" DOMINOES was released late last year to some fairly decent acclaim.

Troy Blackford –

TROY BLACKFORD knows what you did. A fiction writer with a taste for the strange, he has work appearing in places like INKSPILL MAGAZINE, THE MISSING SLATE, THE OVER MY DEAD BODY! Mystery Magazine, CRIME CITY CENTRAL, and BEWILDERING STORIES, among many others. You can also pick up his longer works on Amazon, of which he has eight at the time of this writing, including *Booster & Reeves: The Night of the Revenants*, *Strange Way Out*, *Flotsam*, *Through the Woods*, *Critical Incident*, *For Those With Eyes to See*, and *First There Wasn't, Then There Was*. His website is **www.troyblackford.com** and his stories are all available here.

Thank you for reading 'Robbed of Sleep, Vol 1 – Stories to Stay Up For.' I hope you enjoyed it! If so, please consider leaving a review on Amazon or Goodreads. Every good review helps.

If you liked what you read, and want to be notified the next time one of my strange adventures or anthologies is released, please sign up for my mailing list here:

http://www.troyblackford.com/2013/08/author-updates-mailing-list-for-big.html

Thank you very much, and I hope you have a lot of fun with whatever you read next. Remember: you tacitly agreed to the assumptive proposition of this procedure!

About the Editor

Troy Blackford is a 30 year-old writer living in the Twin Cities with his wife, infant son, and two cats.

His stories have appeared in places like Bewildering Stories, Roadside Fiction, Roar & Thunder, the Glass Coin, Rose Red Review, and Inkspill Magazine.

He has eight publications available on Kindle and in Paperback.

You can find out more about him on his website:
http://www.troyblackford.com